The
Rainbow
CEDAR

Gerri Hill

Bella
BOOKS
2008

Bella Books, Inc.
P.O. Box 10543
Tallahassee, FL 32302

Printed in the United States of America on acid-free paper
First Edition

Editor: Cindy Cresap
Cover designer: LA Callaghan

ISBN-10: 1-59493-124-0
ISBN-13: 978-1-59493-124-6

Thanks to Rosemary Cooper and Melissa Theriot for answering my many questions about Hawaii. As always, a big thank you to Judy Underwood for allowing me to bounce ideas around.

About the Author

Gerri began writing lesbian romance as a way to amuse herself while snowed in one winter in the mountains of Colorado, and hasn't looked back. Her first published work came in 2000 with *One Summer Night*. Many more romances have followed, with the occasional murder mystery in the mix.

Gerri's love of nature and of being outdoors usually makes its way into her stories as her characters often find themselves in beautiful natural settings. When she isn't writing, Gerri and her longtime partner, Diane, can be found at their home in East Texas, where their vegetable garden, orchard and five acres of woods keep them busy. They share their lives with an ever-changing cast of furry friends.

Her favorite pastimes include camping, hiking, birdwatching (though she insists she doesn't wear funny hats yet!), photography and cooking. She collects things nature offers, like an unusual pinecone, colorful rocks or an abandoned bird feather. Dawn is her favorite time of day, the moment right before sunrise . . .

CHAPTER ONE

"Order me a margarita," Jay said. "I'm at the light." She paused and smiled. "And before you say it, yes, I'm the idiot who suggested we come at five o'clock."

She flipped her phone closed and tossed it on the seat beside her, her fingers drumming impatiently on the steering wheel as she waited for the light to turn green. Five o'clock traffic had the downtown area moving at a snail's pace, but she could see the flashing light of her favorite women's bar. Although *bar* was a stretch of the imagination. It was really just a greasy hamburger joint that served the best margaritas in downtown Austin.

Her gaze slipped from the red light to the street, trying to spy a parking spot within a reasonable distance when she spied something much more attractive. Tall and lean—army-green shorts hiding what appeared to be fantastic thighs, and a ball cap pulled low with a short ponytail of brown hair peeking out the back—the woman bent over and slipped her feet into brown leather sandals. *Nice feet. Nice ass.*

A honk behind her signaled the light had turned and Jay pulled forward, glancing to the side for one last look. But her jaw dropped open as the woman pulled her T-shirt off, her bronzed torso glistening in nothing but a bright red sports bra.

"Oh, my *God*," she murmured, her eyes glued to the woman who now held a crisp white tank top in her hands. *She's beautiful.*

But her thoughts—and her movement—were halted as her tiny, gas-saving hybrid plowed into the back of a gas-guzzling truck.

Drew jerked her head around, staring in disbelief as the tiny car rammed the back of her brand new truck before bouncing off.

"Son of a bitch," she muttered. *My truck.* The truck was barely a month old. She tossed the clean white tank on the sidewalk without thinking and rushed to the car.

"Are you okay?"

But she took a step back at the wide, frightened eyes that stared back at her. Wide blue eyes. In fact, the prettiest pair of blue eyes she'd ever seen. *God, she's cute. And she just hit my truck.*

With eyes wide, Jay gripped the steering wheel, her heart pounding rapidly in her chest as she tried to clear her head. "Oh, my *God*," she gasped.

"Are you okay?"

The urgent voice at her window brought her around and she stared dumbly at the woman who looked inside. *Oh, my God.* She shook her head slowly, hoping to be swallowed up by the pavement, or at least hoping the giant truck she'd just run into would continue eating her tiny car, but no such luck.

"Are you hurt?"

Jay shook her head again, then embarrassed herself even further as her gaze locked on the red sports bra.

"I think your door is stuck," the woman said as she pulled on it. Then she stopped and gave a lopsided grin. "Or maybe you could just unlock it? That'd probably help."

Jay could feel her face turning yet another shade of red as she hit the electric locks. The woman pulled the door open and gallantly offered her hand. Jay stared at it for a long moment before placing her own inside.

"I hear these little cars get great gas mileage," the woman said as she helped Jay out. "I don't think they fare too well in crashes though." She led Jay to the sidewalk, then went to survey the damage. "But not too bad." She dropped to her knees and looked underneath the car.

Jay's eyes were glued to her backside.

"No fluids. But I'm not sure I'd chance driving her. The front end is beat to hell."

Jay nodded, her eyes never leaving the woman as she stood again.

The woman came closer, her head tilted to the side. "Do you speak? Or are you in shock?" she asked gently.

"Oh, God," Jay murmured. She stared into her eyes, an odd color of green. Hunter green, she noted. "Can you please put a shirt on?" she asked as she pulled her glance from the red sports bra.

"Oh, of course. I'm sorry. I dropped it over there in all the excitement." She hurried the few feet along the sidewalk to retrieve it. "So, you wanted this parking space pretty bad, huh?"

It was only then that Jay realized her car was parked along the curb, next to a fire hydrant, well out of the line of traffic.

"I'm an idiot." She took a deep breath. "And I need to call the police." She moved to her car, looking for the phone she'd tossed on the seat earlier. It had fallen to the floor from the impact.

"It doesn't look like there's any damage to the truck. Maybe a little ding. I wouldn't bother with the police."

"Well, I'm sure the owner of the truck would like that option," Jay said as she bent to retrieve the phone. "Besides, I think it's required."

"Drew Montgomery. Nice to meet you."

Jay squinted in the sun. "Huh?"

"I own the truck."

Jay bent her head back and stared into the sky, silently cursing herself. "Of course it's your truck. Why *wouldn't* it be your truck?" *Damn my luck today.*

"Huh?"

Jay shook her head. She refused to tell the woman the reason she'd smashed into the back of her. And in all fairness, since it was the woman's fault for practically undressing right there on the street, if she had any sense of decency at all, she'd offer to pay the damages.

"Well, listen, I was about to go over to Rhonda's. Why don't you let me buy you a drink, something to calm your nerves? We can exchange insurance stuff there if you'd like."

"What a coincidence. I was heading to Rhonda's myself."

"One suggestion though. You might want to try to move your car. Kinda close to the fire hydrant there."

Jay looked up and down the street, not seeing another parking spot within the block. "It'll be fine."

Drew shrugged, then led the way over to the bar. Cool air conditioning hit them immediately and Jay unconsciously pulled at her blouse, fanning herself. She found Audrey at their usual table and waved.

"Oh, you're meeting someone," Drew said. "I'm sorry. I should have known."

"Just Audrey, my best friend. I was in need of a therapy session."

"Oh, I see."

4

Jay laughed. "Nothing that serious." She stopped at the table. "Audrey Knor, meet Drew Montgomery."

Jay saw Audrey's eyebrows shoot to the ceiling. Finally, she reached her hand out, shaking Drew's.

"Nice to meet you."

Before Drew could reply, Rhonda came over with a frozen mug, nodding in both their directions.

"Jay, here's your 'rita," she said, placing it on the table beside Audrey. "Drew? Want a beer?"

"Hi, Rhonda. Yes, please." She frowned. "Jay? Is that your name?"

"Oh, I'm sorry. I haven't even introduced myself. Jessica Burns—Jay—everyone just calls me Jay." She pulled out a chair, motioning to another. "Join us."

Drew nodded, glancing at Audrey. "Is that okay with you?"

Audrey looked from one to the other, then frowned. "Wait a minute. Who *are* you?"

Jay laughed. "I'm sorry, Audrey. Drew owns the truck I just hit."

"You hit a truck? With that little tin can you drive? Did it survive?"

"Very funny. That . . . that *tin can* gets sixty miles to the gallon, thank you very much."

"It's going to need a lot of work," Drew supplied. "I was already parked, so I wasn't moving. My truck is fine though. Maybe just a tiny ding in the bumper."

"That's because it's a freakin' tank and gets, what, five miles to the gallon?"

Drew grinned. "Twelve. And it's a diesel."

Audrey leaned forward. "Don't get her started. Everyone's got to have a cause. Jay's is fuel economy."

"Well, it's my work truck. It's my office." At their blank stares, she pulled out a business card from her shorts pocket. "Montgomery Landscaping." She leaned back as Rhonda placed

5

a frosty mug in front of her. "Thanks, Rhonda."

"I've seen your trucks around," Jay said. "You do new subdivisions, right?"

"Yes, mostly. How do you know?"

"I used to work for Wilkes and Bonner Designs."

"Yeah, I've got a contract with Hunt Builders. I think Wilkes and Bonner do too."

"Yes." Jay smiled. "And they're pigs."

Drew laughed. "I see. And you *used* to work for them?"

"I started my own design company. I got tired of doing all the work and getting little credit."

"Or money," Audrey said.

Jay shrugged. "Anyway, Wilkes and Bonner have the majority of the market. They're huge. I've got my cards all over town and can't get a builder to give me the time of day."

"Well, I also have contracts with some smaller independent builders. If you've got some business cards, I'll be happy to recommend you. Not everyone can afford Wilkes and Bonner."

"You would recommend me?" Jay leaned forward, again wondering if those eyes could possibly be that color of green. "You don't know anything about my work. You've not seen my portfolio. I might suck."

Drew raised an eyebrow. "Do you suck?"

"No. I think I'm quite good."

"Okay then. Give me your cards."

Jay opened her purse and pulled out her leather business card holder. She handed over five or six cards, then took one back. "I nearly forgot I hit your truck," she said as she turned the card over, writing quickly. "The number on the front is my cell. This is my home number and address. But you can usually reach me on my cell. I insist on paying to get your bumper repaired."

"It's just a little ding."

"Nonetheless, your truck looks fairly new. Now I've put a dent in it." She handed over the card. "Please. I feel like an idiot for hitting your truck to begin with."

"Yeah. And how did that happen again?"

Jay felt her face flush with embarrassment and quickly looked at Audrey for an escape, but her eyebrows were furrowed as well.

"Really," Audrey said. "I mean, she's parked already and you smash into the back of her? How did that happen?"

Jay scowled at her friend then looked back to Drew with a slight smile. "It's rather embarrassing. And I'd just as soon not share it."

Audrey laughed. "Oh, now you've got to tell us."

Drew took a large swallow of her beer, her smile lighting her face as she nodded. "Please tell. I'm assuming you were distracted," she said, her eyes dancing with amusement.

Jay laughed. "Okay, fine. Yes, distracted. When a beautiful woman such as yourself," she said, pointing at Drew. "When you undress on the sidewalk in broad daylight, there will probably be consequences."

"I wasn't undressing. I was changing shirts."

"In a red sports bra." Jay turned to Audrey. "A nun would have run into the back of her truck."

"Well, a nun, sure. You know what they say about nuns."

Drew laughed. "I'm sorry. If I'd known the sight of me in near undress would cause such havoc, I'd have stayed in my dirty, smelly shirt."

"And boots."

"Don't like sandals?" Drew asked, holding up one leg to show off the offending shoe.

"She's got a foot fetish," Audrey replied and got a swift kick under the table from Jay. "What's that for?"

"Don't like feet?" Drew asked.

"No, no. For some women, it's the breast. Others it's the ass. Jay, she looks at feet."

"Oh, I see."

"Audrey, shut up," Jay hissed. "And I don't have a foot fetish.

7

It's just, you can tell a lot about a person by their feet. And can we please stop talking about this?"

Drew laughed again and Jay stared at her, loving her laugh, loving her eyes. *My God, she's got incredible eyes.* She tore her gaze away, looking someplace safer, looking at Audrey instead.

"I need to get going anyway," Drew said. "I just stopped by to cool off." She shoved her empty mug away, then leaned her elbows on the table. "I've enjoyed meeting you. Both of you," she added with a quick glance Audrey's way. "In fact, maybe we could get together sometime." She met Jay's eyes, holding them. "Dinner?"

"Dinner? Oh, well . . . maybe, sure. Dinner would be—"

Audrey coughed loudly and kicked her ankle under the table.

Jay jerked her head around, staring. Audrey raised both eyebrows. Jay sighed and rolled her eyes. *Katherine.*

"On second thought, maybe I should pass."

Drew leaned back. "Oh. Okay. It's just I thought . . . well, never mind."

She stood to leave but Jay stopped her with a light touch on her arm. "It's just . . . I'm kinda in a relationship. I mean, I *am* in a relationship. Dinner probably wouldn't be a great idea."

"I see. Of course. My apologies." She stood to her full height, taking a step away from the table. "Well, it was still nice to meet you." She leaned closer, smiling. "I can't think of anyone else I'd rather my truck get smashed by."

Jay and Audrey stared at her backside as she walked away, both sighing loudly as the door shut behind her.

"Wow. Dreamy, steamy and creamy all rolled into one."

Jay nodded. "That's crass, but I'll have to agree with you."

"I would hope you'd agree with me. You almost accepted a dinner date with her." Audrey playfully slapped her arm. "Forgot about Katherine, did you?"

Jay laughed. "Yeah, for a minute, yeah." She shrugged. "I haven't actually seen her awake since last Saturday. And that was only for about an hour."

"How does she function? I mean, what's she getting? Like four hours sleep a night?"

"If that. She's completely obsessed with it. If she doesn't make partner, I'm not certain she will survive. But of course she will make partner. That or die trying."

"Have you talked to her? Has it gotten any better?"

Jay shook her head. "No, not better. She was at the office well over a hundred hours last week. It's crazy."

"What's crazy is that you still live together."

Jay sipped from her margarita, glancing at the empty beer mug that Drew Montgomery had been drinking from. She sighed, shoving her drink away from her.

"It occurred to me how dysfunctional that office is," she said. "No one is married. No one has kids." She shrugged. "Well, except for the older Mills. Other than that, no kids. Isn't that strange?"

"Mills?"

"Mills and Mills and Garrett. That's the firm."

"Why did I think it was Bateman and something?"

"Bateman was years ago. She's been with this firm for three years."

"So why does Katherine think she'll make partner?"

"She's brought in tons of clients, tons of money. That's all it takes. Of course, once she makes partner, she'll be working as much if not more, just to prove herself. Old man Mills, well, he thinks women should still be secretaries." She shook her head again. "So, with the encouragement of the younger Mills, Katherine is out to prove him wrong. And I get exhausted just thinking about the hours she puts in."

Audrey grabbed her arm and squeezed. "But Jay, you never see each other. It's been what? Six months?"

"More like eight."

"Damn. How long can you go?"

"I don't know. I mean, we've got nearly eight years together. We have a house, a life. I can't just throw that away, Audrey. She's trying to make good. She's trying to make a name for herself. I have to respect that."

"So you see each other maybe once a week? And you live in the same house?"

"I know. It's crazy. But I keep thinking about how it used to be. We used to have fun. We used to . . . well, we used to be together."

"And now she's a silent partner?"

"Yeah. Although she's going to kill me about this wreck. I'm on her insurance."

"She'll only kill you if she knows why you hit the truck."

Jay grinned, thinking of an excuse. "How about a bee flew in my window? He was buzzing around my head. I lost control."

"Good. Except it's June. Ninety-five degrees out. Why was your window open?"

Jay frowned. "Good point. Okay, how about I swerved to miss a cute little squirrel that had run out in front of me?"

"That's a good one too. But five o'clock traffic, downtown. Don't know how many little squirrels are out and about."

"Damn." Then Jay grinned wickedly. "Okay, some *asshole* nearly hit me! I swerved to avoid him and bam, I hit her truck."

Audrey laughed. "Excellent! That'll fly."

Jay's smile faded as she picked up her nearly empty mug again. "And if I happen to see her on Thursday, I'll tell her that tale."

"So Thursday is still the day for your dinner date?"

"That's how it started. Now it's evolved into her trying to get home before I'm in bed."

Audrey shook her head, then tucked her red hair behind her ears. It was a gesture Jay had learned to recognize in the ten years they'd known each other. Audrey was about to make a profound statement.

"Jay, you have got to talk to her."

"I have talked to her, Audrey."

"No. I mean *really* talk to her. Because this is going to end badly if you don't."

Jay sighed and brushed at her short strands of hair on her forehead. "I talked to her, Audrey." She nodded. "And it was bad, you're right. She accused me of being selfish."

"*What?*"

"I like the prestige—and the money—of her position, but I'm not willing to sacrifice for it. I want the cake and to eat it too, apparently."

"What the hell? You could care less about the *prestige*." She raised her hand to Rhonda. "Bring us another, Rhonda." She looked back at Jay. "That pisses me off. It was her idea to buy that big-ass house. I remember your arguments over that. And your agreement was if she wanted it, she was going to pay for it."

"Right."

"And that's how it still stands?"

"Yes. I mean, we split the bills. But the house payment, yeah, that's all hers." She leaned forward. "Have I told you how much our electric bills were last summer?"

"Yeah. About the same as my monthly rent." They both reached for the frosty mugs at the same time when Rhonda brought over another margarita for them. "Thanks."

"Anyway, we got into a huge fight, accomplished nothing other than having make-up sex, which let me tell you, ain't all it's cracked up to be."

"So now what?"

Jay shrugged. "Nothing. I just needed a therapy session to talk about it, and this," she said, picking up her glass. "Because as you know, I no longer have a social life. You're it, I'm afraid."

"Thanks a lot."

CHAPTER TWO

Drew passed the narrow driveway to her house and drove to the back of the property, parking her truck under the carport she'd built last year. It held three trucks, but everyone knew Drew got the shaded slot at the end. She smiled. One of the perks of being the boss.

Three of her four trucks were back, and she glanced at the numbers, noting Jimmy and his crew was still out. She opened her phone, speed dialing his number as she walked to the back of her truck, her hand moving unconsciously along the smooth bumper, pausing to touch the tiny ding with her index finger.

Damn, she was cute.

"Hey, Jimmy, it's me. Just checking on you. It's after six."

"We're finishing up, Drew. The blueprint was off. We damn near dug up their septic system trying to get that tree in the ground."

Drew nodded. It was a common occurrence with older homes. Some of the blueprints were simply hand-drawn maps marking the septic system and field lines, and sprinkler systems. They had dug up their share of pipes over the years.

"But I trust you *didn't* dig it up."

"Of course not. We moved the tree back about ten feet."

"Need me to call the owner?"

"No. He was here. It's all cool."

"Okay, great. Well, I'm heading up to the house. See you tomorrow."

Drew stepped back and turned a slow circle, her glance going to the trucks and equipment she'd amassed in the last eight years. Her grandparents had left her the house and property, but the business she'd started on her own. Her grandfather had still been alive when she'd started out. For that she was grateful. He'd been so proud.

The youngest of four sisters, all the others being ten years or older than herself, she'd been the only one still living at home when her father had first taken ill. That summer, they shipped her off to Austin to stay with her grandparents, which was fine with her. Nothing but lazy days that seemed to last forever as they alternated between the lake—only a ten-minute drive away—and the spring-fed pool her grandfather had built back in the sixties. After that summer, it became the norm. Each year when school ended, they took her to Austin, and each year, she stayed until the weekend before the new school year began. And when it came time for college, there wasn't much indecision for Drew. She wanted to be in Austin with her grandparents. She just didn't know *what* she wanted to be. So, taking her grandfather's advice, she put off college a year and went to work with him in the tiny plant nursery he'd opened just to keep him busy, her grandmother used to say. But it was there Drew found her calling. So off to college just down the road in San Marcos, she majored in horticulture, a degree her parents and siblings thought she was crazy for getting. How could she possibly make a living with that kind of degree?

She smiled as she turned away from the shop area, as she liked to call it, and headed down the path to the house. It was her grandparents' house, yes, but she'd had it remodeled and redesigned twice now. It hardly resembled the house she remembered. The garden and pool, however, remained nearly as her grandfather had kept it, with only a few modern upgrades. She went there now, closing the wooden gate behind her, locking away the world—and the summer heat—as she walked into the shade, her sandals moving quietly across the flat stones her grandfather had laid by hand nearly fifty years ago. It was one of the things she loved about the pool and garden. No modern-day concrete. Just stones and mortar, a mixture of limestone, hauled down from the Hill Country west of town, and flagstone, smooth flat rock that lined the pool area and provided pathways through the garden. The pool itself, shaped in a curvy S-pattern, was well-shaded now. When she was a kid, the trees were young, the shrubs were barely two feet tall, and flowers had dominated. Today, the pool and garden were kept cool and shaded by the native live oaks her grandfather had planted. Tucked around the trees were flowering mountain laurels and red buds, the showy flowers lasting for weeks during the cool, wet days of April.

The covered sitting area—her addition to the garden—provided all the modern conveniences of an outdoor kitchen, with electricity and running water. She flipped on the ceiling fan, then pulled off her white tank top and tossed it on the wicker loveseat before opening the small refrigerator. She moved the miniature bottles of orange juice aside and selected one of the many varieties of wine coolers she kept there. Standing to her full height, she opened the bottle and took a large swallow, enjoying the refreshing taste of the cool liquid.

Without thought, she slipped off her sandals, then pulled the red bra over her head, tossing it beside her shirt. Her shorts soon followed and she walked confidently to the edge of the pool, her skin shivering in anticipation of the cool spring water. Taking a deep breath, she dove smoothly into the pool, her body gliding just under the surface, taking the curves of the pool with familiar ease. It was a routine she kept to most days, except in the very coldest months of winter. But even then, on occasion, she'd take a quick dip. The water temperature held fairly steady at sixty-six degrees, both winter and summer.

She followed the curves, surfacing only once to take a breath before continuing on to the opposite end, the shallow side closest to the house. There she stopped and stood, seeking out the patch of sunlight as she shook her hair, reminding herself she needed a cut. Then she turned and slipped under the water again, retracing her route to the deep end of the pool. She made five laps, finally stopping and pulling herself out of the pool. She stood there naked, catching her breath, letting the light breeze dry her as she again twisted her hair behind her back, wringing out the water, much like she'd been doing since she was a kid.

In the distance, she heard a truck, knowing Jimmy had made it back. They never came to the house—it was off limits. It was her space and hers alone. The property was only five acres, but it was five acres of prime real estate now. The city had sprawled, growing around her, but she didn't care. The land was her grandfather's and she'd promised him in the beginning she wouldn't sell and let it become gobbled up by some developer who wanted to put up condos or something equally as obnoxious.

She took a clean towel from the cabinet, drying herself, listening as she heard Jimmy's car start and pull away. She was alone again. She sighed. But not for long. She'd agreed to a dinner date. A friend of a friend of a friend. It had sounded like a good idea last week. But today . . . not so much. She was tired. It had been a long, hot day. Then she smiled, remembering the cute blond who'd rammed her truck. *Jay.*

"God, those eyes."

CHAPTER THREE

"No, it didn't damage her truck." Jay rolled her eyes. "And no, she's not going to sue me."

"You never know about people, Jay. They're money-hungry."

Jay walked into the kitchen, eyeing the bottle of wine on the counter. She tucked the phone against her shoulder as she fished for the corkscrew. "I really don't think it's going to be an issue, Katherine. Like I said, it was just a little ding."

"I've seen whiplash proved with less."

Jay poured the wine, watching the burgundy liquid fill the glass. "She wasn't in the truck at the time."

"Well, that's a plus. Look, I'm just swamped, Jay. I'm going to let you handle this. You've got the number to our insurance. If there's even a *hint* of a problem, let me know."

"Of course." Jay paused. "I . . . well, I also got a ticket."

"For what? I thought you didn't even call the police."

Jay chewed her lower lip. "Apparently I was too close to a fire hydrant or something." She rolled her eyes again as she sipped the wine.

"Great," Katherine said dryly. "What's that going to cost you?"

"It wasn't that much," she lied. "I was just concerned about that affecting your insurance as well. Maybe I should just get my own policy."

"It's much cheaper to go through mine. We've been over this before, Jay. Besides they're probably going to total your car. Perhaps you should just use your van for the time being. As old as it is, the insurance is minimal." She sighed. "Now I've really got to run."

"When will you be home?"

"Oh, Jay, I can't even begin to say. What time is it, anyway?"

Jay looked at the clock on the wall. "Nearly nine."

"Already? Well, I've got at least a couple more hours. Did you get dinner?"

Jay nodded. "Yeah, I'm fine. It's just . . . well, I feel like I haven't seen you in a week."

"I know. Please be patient, Jay. I promise, I'll try to make it a short day tomorrow."

Jay nodded again. It was a statement she'd heard daily for months now. So she gave her standard answer, the same one she'd been using for the past three months.

"That'd be nice, Katherine. Maybe we could have dinner together."

"Sure, Jay. Let's plan on it. I'll try not to wake you when I get home."

Jay closed her phone and slid it along the counter, picking up her wine instead. She smiled humorlessly. "Sure, I'll plan on it, Kath. Just like always."

And just like always, she took the bottle of wine with her as she went into her office, closing the door behind her. She always felt better in here. It was *her* space and it reflected her personality. The house—totally Katherine's. But this room, this space, was hers.

Here was where she kept little trinkets and mementoes she'd collected over the years. Here was where she kept her only family picture—that of her grandmother—neatly framed and displayed on the bookshelf. In here was her CD collection, the handful of DVDs she liked to watch over and over, the trashy romance books that Katherine thought she was childish to hang on to, and her most prized possession: a mini Cowboys football helmet autographed by Troy Aikman, Emmitt Smith and Michael Irvin.

She looked affectionately at it, silently counting how many months until football season, her lone sports passion. There was a time, at the beginning, when Katherine would surprise her with tickets to at least one game each season. But the last couple of years, she'd been too busy to even remember Jay's birthday, much less football season.

"Wedded bliss," she murmured, then laughed at her attempt at being sarcastic. It no longer worked.

Jiggling the wireless mouse, she watched the screen saver disappear, replaced with the spreadsheet she'd been working on. She only had two projects going right now, both of which were nearly finished. The spreadsheet was her listing of builders and the contacts she'd made in the last six months or so. The only contractor she had a working relationship with was McGuire and Sons, but they specialized in remodeling, not new homes. He'd pushed some business her way, but she'd found most people—by the time they hired someone to remodel—already had a new design and color scheme in mind. They weren't really interested in her ideas at that stage.

At the bottom of page was the new name she'd added. Drew Montgomery Landscaping. The woman she'd run into yesterday. The woman with the incredible eyes. The woman who said she'd be happy to recommend Jay to some of her builder friends.

Refilling her wineglass, Jay glanced at the business card placed prominently on her desk, a reminder to call after she talked to the insurance company. Of course, a little ding, it might be better to just pay for out of pocket rather than file an insurance claim. Katherine would most likely prefer that, but of course it was her own checkbook that would suffer. A checkbook that could stand to have a few more clients.

She glanced at the clock on her computer, now after nine.

Was it too late?

"Wonder if she lives alone?"

She picked up her phone, flipping it over and over in her hand. Probably lived alone, seeing as she'd asked Jay out. She smiled, pausing to sip from her wine. When was the last time she'd been hit on? Well, it happened occasionally at Rhonda's. But never by someone who looked like Drew Montgomery.

"Oh, hell," she said as she flipped open her phone. She should call her. At least let her know she hadn't forgotten about her truck. After she dialed, she casually tossed the business card back on her desk, leaning back in her chair as she waited. On the fourth ring, just as she expected voice mail to pick up, she heard her voice.

"Drew here."

Jay cleared her throat. "Hi. It's Jay . . . Jessica Burns. The one who hit your truck." She smiled when she heard the quiet laugh on the other end.

"Did you think I would forget you, Jessica Burns? Never."

Jay laughed. "I'm sure there's a dent to remind you. And please call me Jay."

"Okay. And I'm really glad you called. I talked to a builder today. Gave him your card. Seems he's pissed off at Wilkes and Bonner."

Jay sat up straight. "Pissed off? You gave him my card?"

"I don't know all the details, but they outsourced some of

their work, but still charged him as if they did it all. Something like that."

"They used to do that all the time," she said.

"Well, it's R and K Builders. I talked to Randy Kline. He's a good guy." She laughed. "I told him you did killer stuff. I'm assuming your portfolio will back me up?"

"Yes, of course. I really appreciate that, Drew. Especially since you've never seen any of my work."

"No problem. I hate to see the little guy get squeezed. I know how it feels."

"You still consider yourself a little guy?"

"Well, we've grown. Certainly nothing like Apollo Lawns with their fifty or sixty crews. But we're the largest organic landscaping company in the area."

Jay relaxed, leaning back in her chair and refilling her wineglass for the third time. "I had no idea you were organic. How did that start?"

"My grandfather. He had a little nursery out in South Austin, back when South Austin was still outside the city."

"Oh, my God. Montgomery Nursery? I go there all the time."

"Yeah. That was his. They kept the name."

"So—"

"He died seven years ago. But it was the only organic nursery at the time. Bobby Vickers owns it now. He'd worked for my grandfather for years. It was only natural I sell to him. I was too busy with my business to hang on to it."

"Small world," she said quietly.

"That it is. I'm surprised we haven't run into each other before."

"Really. Especially when I worked for Wilkes and Bonner. I was around new construction all the time."

Jay moved from her computer chair to the comfortable recliner tucked into a corner of the office, carefully setting her wineglass on the low table beside it. She was surprised at how at ease she was talking to Drew as their conversation drifted to more personal things, like college and family. But more surprising was how fast the time flew by as they chatted away like old friends.

"Oh, my God, it's after ten," she said later. "I had no intention of taking up this much of your time."

Drew laughed. "And ten is my bedtime on a work night. I don't make exceptions for just anyone, you know."

"And to think I really just called to see about your truck."

"The ding is hardly worth repairing, Jay. I can probably just take it somewhere and have them pop it out of the bumper. Don't go to the trouble of claiming it on your insurance."

Jay paused. "Katherine is afraid you're going to sue."

"Sue? For what? And Katherine is your . . . partner?"

"Yes. She's also an attorney so she's paranoid that way."

"I see. Well, you can tell her I'm not going to sue. It's just a little ding, Jay."

"And I still feel terrible about hitting it. Please promise me you'll let me know the cost when you get it fixed."

"If that'll make you feel better, sure."

"Good. Now I've taken up enough of your time." She stood, stretching out her back. "Go to bed."

Drew closed her phone, unconsciously plugging it in to charge. Normally, she hated talking on the phone. Hated it. State your business, ask your questions, hang up. But tonight the conversation flowed easily. There were no awkward moments, no lulls.

Why are the most interesting women always taken?

"Because they're interesting," she said, stating the obvious.

But she suspected Jay was someone she could become friends with, despite her being in a relationship. They had much in common, and even though their paths hadn't crossed before—professionally—she anticipated them crossing frequently now. Especially if Jay was involved in the interior design of a home when Drew was busy working on the outside.

She finally moved, shoving her thoughts away. It was late and she had a busy day tomorrow.

CHAPTER FOUR

"You know it's already ninety-five out."

"Uh-huh."

Jay nodded at their waiter, nearly ripping the iced tea from his hand and taking a large drink. "God, that's good." She looked at Audrey over the rim of the glass. "Only an insane person would wear pantyhose."

Audrey rolled her eyes. "Not again."

"I'm just saying, skirt and hose? That's archaic."

"Dress code, Jay."

"Which is another archaic concept. Good grief, it's summer." She put the glass down. "In *Texas*."

"I know where we live."

"They shouldn't even *sell* hose during the summer."

"As we've discussed for the last *several* summers . . . brokerage firm, dress code, very important clients. Or have you forgotten where I work?"

"It's insane. That's all I'm saying."

"Why must we have this conversation every summer? Why?"

Jay shook her head. "Because it's insane, and you're making me hot."

Audrey grinned. "Oh, baby. It's been awhile since someone's told me I make them hot."

Jay laughed. "Speaking of hot, I talked to Drew Montgomery the other night."

"Drew? The woman you hit?"

"Yes. We talked for over an hour."

Audrey stared at her. "Now who's insane?"

"It was so easy." Jay leaned back, relaxing. "She put me in touch with a builder. Gave him my card. So I met him this morning. He liked my portfolio, and just like that, I got a job." She smiled as Shelly, Rhonda's lunchtime help, brought their burgers and fries. "Thanks, Shell."

"Shelly? My mayo?"

"Sorry, Audrey. I'll bring it right out."

"She's knows I like mayo," Audrey complained after Shelly was out of earshot. "She knows I dip my fries in mayo. Why doesn't she just bring it out the first time? Why must I *always* ask for it?"

"That's kinda crazy too," Jay said as she shoved two fries into her mouth. "And fattening."

"I have *always* been this size, do not start with me." She paused. "Skinny bitch," she muttered under her breath.

Jay laughed. "I'm sorry. I shouldn't pick on you. You're my only friend."

"Yeah. Try to remember that."

Jay acknowledged the subtle wink Shelly gave her when she returned with the mayo. What started out innocently—forgetting the mayo—had turned into a game for Shelly. One she apparently enjoyed much more than Audrey did.

"I'll try not to forget your tip this time, Shell," Audrey mumbled as she chewed her first fry laden with creamy mayonnaise. "Now, what about this job?"

Jay wiped her mouth with her napkin. "They make the *best* burgers. God. I could eat here everyday."

"You practically do. If I didn't know better, I'd think you were hoping to run into Drew again."

Jay scoffed. "But you *do* know better."

"So, about the job."

"Oh, yeah. It's with R and K Builders. They're a small company. I think they probably only have two or three houses going at once. They're not spec houses. They design them to be custom, so they're really nice. And probably since they are such a small company, Wilkes and Bonner didn't want to waste their talent on them, so they outsourced. Mr. Kline found out and got pissed off," she said, remembering Drew's words. Randy Kline, when they'd met, said no such thing.

"So what'd you get? Just one house?"

Jay grinned. "That's the great part. I think he intended to give me one house, just to try me out. But he *loved* my portfolio. In fact, he said my style was just what he was looking for." She knew she was beaming, but she couldn't help it. "I got *three*."

"Oh, wow, Jay, that's fabulous. I'm so proud."

Jay reached across the table and squeezed Audrey's hand. "Thanks. I feel like maybe—finally—my big break is here."

"So why don't we go out and celebrate tonight?" Audrey bit into her burger, chewing quickly. "Or is Katherine making herself available, since it is Friday and all?"

"I haven't even told Katherine yet." Jay stood. "I'm going to get us some more tea." At the counter, she winked at Shelly as she grabbed a half-full pitcher of tea and brought it back to their table. "Besides, Friday nights are no different than any other night for her."

Audrey shook her head, but Jay wasn't in the mood to listen

to how bad Katherine was. She didn't need Audrey to tell her.

"So, what'd you have in mind?"

"See a movie?" Audrey suggested.

Jay thought for a moment, then shook her head. "I'm too wired to sit still that long."

"Dancing?"

"Good grief, no. You and me?" Jay glanced at the blackboard behind the tiny stage, noting one of her favorite singers was playing tonight. She hadn't been out to listen to Tammy George since last summer. "How about margaritas?"

"That means here."

"Tammy George."

Audrey whipped her head around, her eyes wide as she read the board. "Wow. Cool." She nodded. "Okay, but it'll be crowded."

Jay knew it would, but it would be fun. A night out. And she knew Katherine wouldn't mind. She suspected it was a load off Katherine's mind knowing Jay had a pal like Audrey. Audrey was forever single, but forever looking. She went on her share of blind dates, but—as Jay had told her once—she was looking for a diamond among a box full of rocks. Therefore, one blind date rarely led to two, which was why Audrey had as much free time on her hands as Jay did.

"Crowded is fine," Jay said as she picked up her burger again. "Besides, maybe you'll get lucky."

Audrey snorted. "I've been here when it's crowded. They come out of the woods. And frankly, most of the women who come out of the woods scare me." She dipped a fry into her mayo cup, then pointed it at Jay. "But might you be hoping it's crowded enough for a Drew Montgomery sighting?"

"Oh, don't be silly," Jay said, dismayed to feel her face flushing with embarrassment. The thought had crossed her mind, she admitted.

"Right. And I'll just pretend I didn't see you blush."

"Oh, all right," she conceded. "Would it be so bad if she were here? I need to thank her anyway. My new job and all."

"You could just call her. Because as much as I hate what Katherine is doing to you, I think this Drew person is going to be trouble."

"Trouble? How so?"

Audrey raised her eyebrows. "Dreamy, steamy and creamy."

CHAPTER FIVE

"Good God, you're right," Jay said as she clung to Audrey's arm. "Where did all these women come from?" Their normally quiet bar was hopping with wall-to-wall bodies, the noise level reaching a raucous decibel.

"Tammy George is cute, talented, rich and single," Audrey said loudly. "And most everyone here would dump their girl-friend to be with her."

"Oh, that's insane. I love her music, yeah. And she is kinda cute—"

"Kinda? What rock are you living under?"

"But she's not relationship material. And how can she be? She travels all the time. Unless you went with her, you'd never get to see each other. How can she ever have any kind of relationship?" Jay came to an abrupt stop as Audrey spun around.

"Did you even hear what you just said?"

Jay blinked several times, then narrowed her eyes. "What are you insinuating?"

"I'm just asking if you heard the words that came out of your mouth? About not being able to have a relationship when you don't get to see each other. Those words."

"Shut up, Audrey. No therapy session tonight, please?" Jay tucked her hand in the crook of Audrey's elbow, leading her through the crowd of women, trying to find the bar. "God, I hope Shelly's here tonight. I don't even recognize half the people working the bar."

"There's Rhonda."

Audrey shoved her way between three women, pulling Jay with her to the bar. Rhonda greeted them with a huge grin.

"Can you believe this place?" she asked as she refilled a bowl with peanuts. "We'll run out before the night is through."

Jay grabbed a handful and began cracking the shells. "What are the chances of getting a 'rita?"

"Gotta keep my regulars happy, don't I? Coming right up."

Jay turned around and leaned against the bar, scanning the crowd. A few familiar faces, that was all.

"Tammy George is in her mid-thirties. What are all these young kids doing here?" Audrey asked above the music.

Jay rolled her eyes. "So now that you're twenty-nine, you feel old?"

Audrey made a face. "I just don't have anything in common with twenty-one-year olds."

"Rhonda needs to have live music more often. This place has an energy tonight, doesn't it?"

"Yeah, young sweaty bodies in heat will do that."

Jay turned, her witty comment forgotten as her eyes locked with a pair of green ones across the room. Drew Montgomery. Seconds passed, then Drew nodded slightly before turning her attention to an attractive woman beside her.

"God, she is so *damn* cute," she murmured.

"What'd you say?" Audrey asked loudly.

Jay grabbed her arm and squeezed. "She's here."

"She? She who?"

"Who do you think?"

"Drew?"

Jay spun around, her back to the crowd. "She's got a date."

"Did you think she wouldn't?"

"No, I'm just saying she's here with someone so I doubt we'll even talk."

"Think again."

Jay turned back to the crowd, her eyes widening as Drew Montgomery headed their way. She smiled in greeting, wishing she wasn't quite so happy to see her.

"Hi, ladies," she said loudly, just before a roar from the crowd as band members took the stage. "Good to see you again."

Before she could stop herself, Jay grabbed Drew's arm and pulled her closer. "I got a job," she nearly yelled.

"So I heard. He loved your stuff."

Jay laughed. "I know. Thank you so much for doing that."

But Drew shook her head. "All I did was hand him your card. Nothing to thank me for."

"Well, I can't wait to get started. First thing Monday."

"Then maybe we'll run into each other. I've got those same three houses."

"You want a drink?" Audrey interrupted. "Rhonda's coming this way."

Drew declined. "I should get back. I don't suppose I'm making a very good impression on a first date, standing here talking to two beautiful women." She winked at Jay. "Maybe I'll see you next week."

Before Jay could reply, Drew had disappeared into the crowd, leaving Jay staring after her. *She's just perfect. Beautiful, charming . . . perfect.*

"Yo, earth to Jay."

"Hmm?"

"You're married."

Jay sighed. Yes. Married. "She's just so . . . so beautiful." Jay glanced back over the crowd but didn't spot Drew. "I mean . . . simply gorgeous."

"True." The band started up and the crowd roared as Tammy George walked out. Audrey leaned closer, speaking directly into her ear. "But you have Katherine."

And where was Katherine? Was she even aware it was Friday night? Did she know that Jay was out at the bar? Would she even care?

Katherine was at the office, and no, she didn't know it was Friday, didn't know where Jay was . . . and no, she probably didn't care.

So Jay picked up her fresh margarita and took a sip, letting her eyes close for a brief few seconds as the music penetrated. She then turned into the crowd, her head bobbing to the beat, her gaze landing on Tammy George. Yes, she was definitely attractive, just oozing with raw energy. But as Tammy's hips gyrated and swayed, Jay felt very little. She glanced at Audrey, whose gaze was locked on the singer's every move, as were most of the others in the bar. Jay felt a curious sense of disconnection, of alienation. She felt there was a place she belonged, but it wasn't here. A heaviness settled over her, the crowd becoming nearly claustrophobic as her eyes darted across the bar, women moving in unison to the music. The room seemed to take on a life of its own, expanding and breathing as the crowd of women bobbed and swayed, all eyes on Tammy George.

She quickly set her drink on the bar, grabbing Audrey's arm and pulling her closer. "I gotta get some air," she said loudly.

Audrey nodded, her gaze turning back to the stage as Jay slipped quickly away.

CHAPTER SIX

Jay stood in the middle of the room, holding swatches up, trying to decide on which shade of brown to go with. Earlier, after much indecision, she'd chosen a rusty red for the walls in the dining room, but the contrast for the baseboards and trim was proving a difficult choice. Mainly because she hated rusty red.

"Then why did you choose it?" she asked, her low voice echoing in the empty house.

Yesterday, as she finished up the faux painting in the living room—her specialty—she'd had to fight the last of the carpenters as they'd finished staining the cabinets in the kitchen. Today, she was completely alone, and she'd gone from room to room, picking out colors and designs. Tomorrow she'd start the actual painting. Connie, whom she met while still at Wilkes and Bonner, served as her part-time help, quite happy to slap paint on walls all day while she sang along with her iPod. Which was fine with Jay. She could play with faux painting for hours, but when it came to uniform colors, she got bored with it easily.

Which was what she was fast approaching as she tried to decide on this, her last room.

"Whatcha doin'?"

Jay jumped, her scream turning into a growl, watching hundreds of swatches fall to the floor as her hand went to still her racing heart. Drew Montgomery stood there, tiny tank top barely covering her upper body, loose-hanging shorts stained with dirt covering the lower portion. Jay couldn't help herself as her gaze moved over the woman, pausing at her feet, which were safely clad inside work boots.

She finally breathed again. "You scared the *crap* out of me," she said, breaking into a smile.

"Sorry, didn't mean to. Thought you heard me." Drew bent to gather the fallen swatches and Jay did the same. "Hope these weren't in any particular order."

"Every good designer would tell you of course they're in some sort of order." Jay grinned. "I have a hard time keeping them that way." She paused. "You're starting on the yard?" Mr. Kline had told her Drew would be by sometime this week, not that Jay had been looking for her or anything.

"Yeah. Should have been here Monday, but we got behind. We were about half done with this other house when it sold. The new owner wanted some things changed."

"Can they do that?"

"Oh, sure. If they want to pay. The builders have already paid me and have tacked on the cost of landscaping into the price of the house. That won't change. But the new owners can plant whatever they want. I certainly don't want to go to the trouble of putting in my stuff only to have them rip it up. So I try to work with them on the cost."

They stood, Drew handing Jay her share of the swatches.

"Thanks," Jay said, allowing Drew to capture her eyes. Now she knew why she'd picked that particular color of green for the master bedroom. It just oozed sexuality.

"I better get busy. I don't hear any work going on so I guess the guys are waiting on me."

"Okay, yeah. I should finish up too."

"Oh? You're already done for the day?"

Drew sounded disappointed and Jay shook her head. "Just with picking out the last of the colors. Then it's shopping for paint."

"You don't do all this yourself, do you?"

"Any type of faux painting, yes. But I have someone who helps me with wall painting. She's a college graduate with a degree in petroleum engineering who doesn't want to leave Austin." Jay shrugged. "And she works for fifty cents more than minimum wage."

"Quite the bargain then," Drew said with a laugh. She headed for the door, then paused. "If you're up for it, we could swing by Rhonda's for a drink later."

It was said so casually, so *friendly*, Jay couldn't think of any reason to decline. So she smiled and nodded. "I'd love it."

"Great."

Jay watched her go, her gaze glued to her backside as she bounded down the steps and out into the yard. It *was* hot, she reasoned. A cold margarita would go down nicely after work. She spun around, a grin on her face. She shouldn't have accepted, she knew. But Drew Montgomery wasn't someone she could resist.

She stopped short, her smile turning into a frown. *Resist?* Oh, of course she could resist her. That wasn't what she meant. It was just . . . well, it *was* hot out.

"I never saw you again. Did you slip out early?" Drew asked as she settled into the booth opposite Jay. She'd changed shirts—

34

in the privacy of her truck this time—before joining Jay on the sidewalk. And despite Jay's attempt to look disinterested, Drew saw her glance into the cab of the truck many times. She knew Jay was in a relationship, knew she wasn't interested in her, but still, sometimes when Jay looked at her, she had the impression Jay was fighting with herself.

"I got claustrophobic. I don't know what it was. All those women, all that noise." Jay waved her hand dismissively. "I just needed some air."

"Yeah. It was a bit crowded. Years ago, I used to love Tammy George. But she's gotten older, I've gotten older. She just doesn't do anything for me anymore."

Jay laughed. "I know what you mean. I was thinking the same thing." Jay leaned closer. "And all those young girls there. How do they even know who Tammy George is?"

"Well, she's still attractive and she can still rock."

"And apparently draw a crowd."

Drew paused, waiting while Rhonda brought their drinks over. A margarita for Jay and a beer for her.

"Here you go, ladies. Chips and salsa, on the house. Enjoy."

"Thanks, Rhonda."

Drew smiled as she watched Jay reach for her drink, the audible sigh turning into a satisfied groan.

"God, that's good." Jay looked up. "I think I'm addicted to them."

Drew held up her beer. "I've never developed a taste for tequila." She grinned. "And don't tell anyone, but I have a fondness for fruity drinks."

"Would ruin your image, would it?"

"Oh, absolutely." Drew shoved a chip into her mouth after scooping up salsa.

"How was your date the other night? You said it was a first one," Jay asked.

"She's the friend of a girlfriend of a friend of mine."

"Huh?"

Drew laughed. "My friend Val, her girlfriend is good friends with her. Sheila."

"Oh. And how did that work out?"

"It was okay. She's a bit young for me, I think. She wanted to go bar-hopping at straight clubs after Tammy George. Frankly, I couldn't keep up. I doubt there'll be a second date."

"Do you have these blind dates often?"

"Far too often, I'm afraid. Friends can't stand to see me single and can't understand how I can be content going home to an empty house every night." She held up her empty beer mug to Rhonda, then glanced at Jay's glass, still half full. "But I work hard during the week. I'm usually too exhausted for dating."

"And why exactly are you still single?"

Drew tilted her head. "What kind of question is that?"

"You're attractive, you own your own business. Why hasn't someone latched on to you?" Jay grinned. "Or do you have some really annoying habits that run them off?"

"Not that I'm aware of. But at this stage in my life, I'm not out just looking for a good time. You can get that anywhere. I've got this image in my mind of the type of woman I'd like to spend my life with." She leaned forward. "Certain qualities that appeal to me. And so far, I've not found her. And so I'm content going home to an empty house. I don't want to just settle."

"What are you? Mid-thirties?"

"Yeah. Thirty-six. You?"

"Thirty-two." Jay twirled her glass, then looked up, meeting Drew's eyes. "Can I ask you something personal?"

Drew nodded.

"I love your name. But *Drew* . . . where did it come from?"

Drew laughed. "When you said you wanted to ask me something personal, I thought it was going to be about my love life."

"I don't know you *that* well yet." Jay took a chip, skipping the salsa.

"I see." Drew took her beer from Rhonda. "Thanks."

"Are you ladies staying for dinner?"

"Oh, no," Jay said. "Just a drink."

"Very well. If you want something to snack on other than chips, let me know."

"Thanks, Rhonda." Jay looked back to Drew. "Your name?"

"My name. Well, I'm the youngest of four girls. My father is Andrew, one of five Andrews in his family, cousins and all. I was the last shot at a boy." She shrugged. "I would have preferred Andi instead of Drew though."

Jay shook her head. "Andi is too . . . too cutesy. Like Candi, or Toni, or something. Drew suits you better. It's stronger."

"Well, my father would be happy. Thank you." Their eyes held for a moment, and again Drew was confused by what she saw there. If this was any other woman, not one who was in a long-term relationship, she'd acknowledge the attraction, acknowledge the subtle undercurrents of electricity that flowed between them. But this was Jay, a woman she'd talked to a handful of times, a woman she'd asked out to dinner and was told a polite no, she was in a relationship. So, Drew dismissed those thoughts and instead gave in to her own curiosity. "What about your name? Jay?"

"Oh, nothing exciting. In fact, I hated it at first. I was Jessica, which suited me just fine. But in high school, there were three of us, so obviously, nicknames abounded. Jay just stuck with me." She laughed. "In fact, no one ended up with Jessica. There was Jess, there was J.C., and then me, Jay."

"Where was high school? Are you from Austin?"

Jay smirked. "Lubbock."

"Ouch."

"Yeah. The armpit. But I stayed there long enough for a couple of years of college. And then, well, things happened."

Drew raised an eyebrow. "Family?"

"Yeah, family. There was no boyfriend. It started to raise

37

questions. So much so that my brother started following me around. It didn't take long to figure things out, you know."

"I'm sorry."

"There was no happy ending. And I know it happens a lot, I just never thought it would happen to me. I never imagined my father chasing me out of the house, waving a Bible at me. I'm totally estranged from my family still. I've not tried to contact them since I left, and as far as I know, they've not tried to find me."

"Wow. That's sad. One brother, that's it?"

"A younger sister. We were close. And my grandmother. I was really close with her. I called her after it happened, in tears, but she hung up on me." Jay stared at her empty glass for a moment before looking up. "I was twenty when I left, so it's been a while. But my grandmother, that hurt. She was special to me. I guess I miss her the most."

Drew nodded. "I don't see my family much, but it's not because we're estranged or anything. They're all still down in Houston. And when I get a break from work and want to get away, Houston isn't it," she said with a smile. "I make a point to get down for Christmas though."

"They never come here?"

"My folks come every so often. My dad's health isn't great. My sisters, no. They're all married with a bunch of kids. They're big-city girls. They think of Austin as just a college town still. The last time they were here was when my grandfather died."

"I miss having a family," Jay said. She looked around for Rhonda, holding up her empty glass with a smile. "I shouldn't have another, but what the hell."

"But you've got your own family now, right?"

Jay frowned. "What do you mean?"

"Katherine?" Drew raised an eyebrow as a faint blush crept over Jay's face.

"Right, Katherine." Jay nodded. "Sure. I mean, we've been

together eight years. It's just, well, she works so much, I hardly ever see her. The last year, anyway."

Drew nodded, not knowing what to say.

"But yeah, she's my only family, really. And Audrey, she's been my rock. She's always there."

"Your therapist?"

Jay laughed. "Right. My therapy sessions."

Drew met her gaze, holding her eyes captive for a moment. "Well, if you're adding friends to your life, I hope you'll consider me. Because I really enjoy your company."

CHAPTER SEVEN

Jay tossed her keys on the bar, still surprised at the time. Their quick drink had turned into two, along with a plate of nachos they shared. And they'd talked. And talked. She couldn't understand why she enjoyed being around Drew so much. It went past the physical attraction she felt.

"Whoa," she said out loud. *Physical attraction?* Sure, Drew was cute, charming. But it wasn't like she was attracted to her in *that* way. Not seriously, anyway. She'd teased with Audrey about it, that was one thing. Just teasing.

Because there was Katherine.

"Right. There's Katherine."

And here it was, eight thirty in the evening and her phone never rang. There was no concerned call from Katherine wondering why they hadn't talked all day. No call to check on her, and no call just to say hello. Jay tilted her head, trying to remember the last time they did talk. Yesterday? No, they'd only exchanged voice mail. Sunday, Jay had a vague memory of Katherine in bed with her but that was all. She'd spent the morning in her office picking through swatches, and had spent the afternoon with Audrey at Barton Springs pool. And Saturday, the day after she'd left the bar early, she'd been in no mood for anyone's company and hadn't even considered complaining to Katherine about their lack of time together. When she got home from the bar Friday night, the house was dark and empty. She'd gone straight to bed. Katherine had come home at two in the morning, had crawled into bed after her shower and had attempted to wake Jay, wanting to make love. Jay had simply rolled away and drifted off to sleep again. When she woke, Katherine was already gone.

So she made her way up the stairs, past their bedroom and into her tiny office. She shut the door behind her as if that could shut out the reality of what her life had become. What she'd told Drew was true. Katherine *was* her only family. For eight years, there was always just Katherine. Oh, they had a small circle of friends, but no close, close friends. No one she'd consider donating a kidney to or anything. And for Jay, there was Audrey. This last year, she couldn't even fathom what her life would have been like if not for Audrey.

But again, that feeling of not belonging, that nagging feeling that left her stomach tied in knots, that feeling of apprehension, of uneasiness settled over her. She felt nearly disconnected with her world as she moved to her recliner, leaning back and closing her eyes.

Alone. That was all she was.

Alone.

CHAPTER EIGHT

"You know, we've done this a hundred times, Drew. You don't need to supervise," Johnny told her days later as they planted shrubs around the front of the house.

"I'm not supervising. I like doing this sort of thing."

"You hate shrubs."

Drew stood and wiped the sweat from her brow. "Yeah. Shrubs are boring." She grinned. "So I'll let you guys finish and I'll go inside the house—where I hear the AC running—and see if Jay will let me wash up."

"I thought we weren't supposed to *ever* set foot inside a new house. What happened to that rule?"

"That rule still applies to you, Johnny. But since I make the rules, I can break them."

Johnny laughed. "So I'll guess that if it were, say Frankie Mason from Wilkes and Bonner in that house, you wouldn't be so interested in going inside four or five times a day."

"Jay has a distinct advantage over Frankie Mason, yes. But it's not like you think. She's attached. We're just friends."

"Yeah, just your luck, huh?"

Drew's smile faded. Yeah, just her luck. She and Jay were quickly becoming friends. They were comfortable in each other's presence. Conversation never lacked. And always, that underlying degree of attraction was there, both of them ignoring it as far as Drew could tell. Jay rarely spoke of Katherine. In fact, sometimes Drew wondered if Jay forgot that Katherine existed.

But it didn't matter. Drew knew her limitations as far as Jay was concerned. Friends. Nothing more. And that was enough. Although Jay never said, she suspected Jay craved Drew's friendship as much as Drew did Jay's. She couldn't explain it. It was just there. From the moment they met, from the moment Jay ran into her truck and Drew had looked in her eyes, it was there.

So that's why Drew now bounded up the steps, pausing to remove her dirty boots before going inside.

"You don't think it's too dark?" Jay turned in a circle, looking at the walls, then back at Connie. "Too much red?"

"It's the latest thing."

"How can you possibly enjoy a meal with all this red?"

"People use their formal dining rooms maybe three times a year," Connie stated. "And a nice table and chairs with red velvet cushions would match nicely."

"Well, I hate it."

"Me too."

Jay turned, surprised to find Drew standing there watching them. She smiled. "Hey, you. You hate it, huh?"

"A little on the red side."

"It's supposed to be," Connie said.

"In fact, it's so red, it might be the deciding factor in *not* buying the house."

Jay nodded. "I agree." She turned to Connie. "We've got to tone it down some. How about a light burgundy?"

"Beige trim?"

"We could do a beige trim with just a *hint* of burgundy to match. Right?"

"The last time we tried just a *hint* of something, remember what happened?"

Jay laughed and glanced at Drew. "We ended up with puke green. It was disgusting. No matter what we did, the walls were still puke green." Jay walked by Connie, lightly squeezing her shoulder. "Give it a try, okay?" She took Drew's arm and led her out of the room. "She's the creative sort," she whispered when they were out of earshot. She let her hand slip off Drew's arm, silently cursing her need of physical touch. Instead, she folded her hands under her arms, watching Drew. "What's up?"

Drew ducked her head, a slight flush marring her features. "Nothing. Just wanted to cool off."

"I see. Taking advantage of the AC? And as boss you can do that." She glanced at Drew's feet. "And you were kind enough to take off your boots."

Drew followed her gaze to her dirty socks. "I don't suppose these are much cleaner," she said as she wiggled her toes.

"You want to wash up?"

"You read my mind?"

"You're filthy."

"It's part of my charm."

"That it is," Jay said before she could stop herself. She met Drew's eyes quickly, then looked away. She pointed down the hall. "Use the spare bathroom. I have towels in there already." She watched as Drew walked—sauntered—away from her. "Just ignore the paint stains," she called after her. She spun around, clenching her fists together, *hating*, absolutely *hating* her attraction to Drew. They could be good friends. Really, they could be.

Couldn't they?

Would it be like it was with Audrey? Could she tell Drew anything and expect nothing but support from her? Could she sleep over at her house when Katherine was away and stay up talking half the night?

She rolled her eyes. *Right.*

No, she wasn't stupid. Neither was Drew. And if she wasn't careful—if they *both* weren't careful—they would end up totally screwing up their budding friendship.

"Hey."

Jay spun around again, finding Drew watching her. She fell into her eyes, not even trying to stop herself. She simply couldn't help it. No woman should have eyes that color. "Hunter green," she murmured.

Drew frowned. "Huh?"

"Your eyes," Jay said quietly. "I love your eyes."

Drew nodded. "I kinda like yours too."

Jay swallowed with difficulty, finally turning away, her back to Drew. "I should get back to it, I suppose."

"Yeah, me too."

Drew moved closer. Jay could feel her. She stopped breathing.

"I won't be around tomorrow, Jay."

Jay turned, eyebrows raised.

"Got another yard to start on."

Jay nodded. "Okay."

"Want to maybe go to Rhonda's afterward?"

Jay looked away. She should decline, she knew she should. *Just say no.* But like any drug addict, she couldn't. "Okay."

Drew tilted her head. "Or maybe Katherine will be waiting on you?"

Jay's quick laugh was bitter, but she couldn't stop it. "No, Katherine will definitely *not* be waiting on me."

"When are you ever going to tell me about that?"

"Tell you what?"

"About Katherine. You seem to have a lot of free time." She moved closer. "If I were Katherine, I would be home every day at five, just to be with you. But something keeps her away."

Oh God, did Drew not have any idea what her presence did to her? "Katherine's trying to make partner. She works like a thousand hours a week. We hardly see each other," Jay said. Actually, that was a stretch. They hardly *spoke* these days.

She moved away from Drew, walking purposefully back to the dining room and Connie, where it was safe, where they wouldn't be alone.

"So you want to get a burger then?"

Jay nodded. "Sure. Call me when you're decent."

Drew laughed. "I may not be able to wash up. You may have to deal with a smelly me with a clean shirt."

"Just as long as you change before you get there." Jay stopped. "Wait a minute. You never told me what I owe you for the ding."

"Nothing, I told you."

"And I told you I was going to pay for it."

"Well, there's nothing to pay for. I haven't gotten it fixed."

"Why not?"

"I decided I liked it."

They looked at each other, both staring. "You like the ding?" Drew nodded.

Jay smiled. "I think you want to leave it so you'll have something to hold over my head."

"Perhaps." Drew moved to the door, pausing. "See you tomorrow. I'll call you."

"Can't wait."

Sadly, it was the truth. With a sigh, she turned to Connie, finding her watching. "What?"

"She's cute."

"I know."

"Really cute."

"I know."

"She's got a thing for you."

Jay shook her head, about to deny it, but didn't. "I know," she said instead.

"And it goes both ways, I suspect."

Jay took a deep breath, letting it out slowly. "Yes, I know."

CHAPTER NINE

"I need a therapy session."

"I thought you were cured. I haven't heard from you all week."

"Want to come over? We could swim."

"To the mansion? No, thanks."

Jay laughed. "I'd suggest Rhonda's, but I've been there three times this week."

"And who are you stepping out with?"

Jay bit her lower lip. "Drew."

"Oh, my God," Audrey practically yelled into the phone. "Are you insane?"

"Like I said, I need a therapy session."

"Come to the apartment. We'll order pizza."

"You're a peach. Be right there."

Jay folded her phone and tossed it onto the seat. What she

really wanted was for Audrey to talk her out of her dinner date tomorrow night. Well, no, what she *really* wanted was for Audrey to say it was okay to have dinner with Drew. It was just burgers at the bar, after all.

"Right. Audrey will be all over that one," she said sarcastically.

She drove quickly, taking the exit off of MoPac and going to West Lake Hills. Their own home, tucked into the hills near Balcones, was but a stone's throw across the hills. But here in apartment hell, it was hard to imagine the tranquility of their spacious cedar and oak lot. Not that Audrey's apartment complex lacked character. It was better than most, with native trees tucked into every available spot, trying to hide the concrete and pavement that had ruined it to begin with.

She hurried through the parking lot, the summer heat still permeating as the asphalt shimmered even after the sun had slipped below the trees. She rapped on the door, waiting for Audrey to unlock it and let her in. Cool air hit her face as she slipped inside and she slumped back against the door, fanning herself.

"I hate summers."

"You weren't complaining the other day when we were at the pool."

"That's different. Barton Springs pool is a ritual." She shoved off the door and tossed her purse on the sofa, following Audrey into the kitchen, spying the blender on the counter. "Gonna make margaritas?"

"Yep. Got a new mix."

"Fabulous. But what was wrong with your old one?"

"Nothing. This is just different." Audrey bent down, finding the tequila bottle. "And guess what? I've got a date tomorrow night."

Jay grinned. "You do? Wonderful. Who with?"

"Her name is Diante."

"Diante? What the hell kind of name is that?"

Audrey shrugged. "Don't know. I just met her at a meeting today. She's a banker." Audrey paused. "Older than me. She's probably in her forties."

"A banker in her forties who is single?" Jay raised her eyebrows. "She *is* single, right?"

"She's from Dallas. Only in town this week."

"So does that mean she's single?"

Audrey shrugged again. "I didn't ask. I mean, I guess she's single if she asked me out."

"Maybe it's just dinner. Not really a date."

"No, I think it's a date."

Jay's eyes widened. "She wants to have sex?"

"That was the gist I got."

"But you don't do that."

Audrey laughed. "Of course I have sex."

"Not with strangers. You don't have sex with strangers," Jay insisted.

"Okay, Jay. I don't have sex with strangers."

"Oh, my God! You're going to *sleep* with her. You just met her today."

"I swear, you're such a prude. She's a professional woman, quite attractive I might add, and in town for a week. It's not any concern of mine if she's single or not."

"You wore that short skirt, didn't you," Jay accused.

"With fishnet hose. She didn't stand a chance."

"You're so bad. Perhaps you're the one in need of a therapy session."

The doorbell rang and Audrey stopped Jay as she went to her purse. "It's on me this time."

Jay took the pizza back to the bar, pulling out a bar stool and flipping open the box before Audrey had even paid.

"You've not eaten today?"

Jay shook her head. "Not a bite," she said with her mouth full.

Audrey poured ice into the blender and pushed the button. Jay watched the ice spin, her mouth watering as she waited for Audrey to finish.

"Try this," Audrey said, sliding a glass her way. "It's got more of a lime tang to it."

Jay took a sip, nodding. "Good. Different, but good."

"Thought you'd like it." Audrey pulled out a bar stool and joined Jay, picking up a piece of pizza. "I only had a salad for lunch. Pizza sounded good."

"I'm not used to working, I guess," Jay said. "I need to start making a sandwich or something. By the time you drive somewhere to eat and get back, you've lost nearly two hours."

"So, what about this therapy session?"

Jay put her pizza down and reached for her drink instead. "I've been to lunch with her. And we went to the bar for drinks the other day after work. But we didn't have dinner, just a plate of nachos."

"So what's got you worried?"

"She asked me to meet her there for dinner tomorrow."

"And you said?"

Jay looked away. "I said yes."

"Jay, Jay, Jay. You are just looking for trouble, aren't you?"

"We're friends. There's nothing wrong with having dinner. You and I do it all the time."

"A bit different."

"How so?"

"You don't cream your pants every time you see me."

"Oh, that is *so* gross," Jay said with a laugh. "And so not true."

"What? You do cream your pants when you see me?"

Jay nearly spit out her drink. "No! You know what I mean. Besides, Drew knows about Katherine. She knows it's just friendship between us."

"She may know that Katherine exists in your life, but does she know how this last year has been? Does she know Katherine has been absent for the last eight months? Does she know how unhappy you are?"

Jay stared at her. "I'm not unhappy."

"Oh, Jay, you don't have to say it for me to know. You're miserable. You had an anxiety attack the other night, didn't you?" Audrey gripped her hand. "When you left the bar?"

Jay nodded.

"If you feel like your relationship with Katherine is failing, spending time with Drew is not going to solve anything. It'll just make it worse."

"Worse for whom?"

"For everyone, Jay. Katherine may be totally blinded by this. She may have no idea how unhappy you are. In fact, I'd swear to it. She's not around enough to know. And knowing you, you've not told her. You just go along with this crazy plan of hers, letting her work herself into an early grave, just to make partner at a firm long known for its suppression of women. Good grief, with her reputation, she could probably go to any firm in town and name her price. But no, she wants to prove something, wants to be the first."

"It's crazy, I know."

"So you've got to tell her. I know you've said you talked, but have you really told her how miserable you've been?"

"How can she not know? My God, we see each other less than roommates would." Jay got up to refill her glass. "And the other night, she comes home well after midnight—nearly two—and wants to have sex."

"And you didn't?"

"No." She took a deep breath. "I don't. I mean, I have such . . . such *anger* inside me. How can she not see that? Doesn't our relationship mean anything to her? Doesn't it mean more than her goddamn career?"

Audrey's eyebrows shot up and Jay smiled apologetically. "Sorry. I know you hate that word."

"So, you're angry at Katherine for the deterioration of your relationship?"

"Yes."

"And that's where Drew comes in?"

Jay shook her head. "No. I don't have any romantic interest in Drew. I like her. I enjoy her company. And I don't see anything wrong with having dinner with her."

"You're so full of shit. Fill me up," Audrey said as she handed Jay her glass. "So if you see nothing wrong with it, then why are you here wanting me to give you my blessing?"

"Because I feel guilty," Jay said.

"Why?"

"Because . . . *damn*, she's cute and attractive and . . . and perhaps I am a little bit attracted to her."

"A little?"

"Okay, a lot. Jesus, you're good at this," Jay said with a laugh.

"There, we've got it out in the open finally. You're attracted to Drew, you feel guilty for seeing her, and what else?"

"I swear, Audrey, sometimes I hate you."

"What are friends for?"

"So I shouldn't go to dinner with her, right?"

Audrey laughed. "We both know you're going to dinner with her. But I think you need to decide how far you're going to take it. I think you should be honest with her. Tell her about Katherine, and tell her you're attracted to her."

"Are you crazy? I will not."

"Why?"

"Because, that's why. Because."

"Because you know she's attracted to you too? Because if you admit it to her, then who knows what will happen?"

"Oh, Audrey . . . yes and yes." Jay put her glass down and paced, moving behind Audrey. "Yes, we have this *thing*. I know it. She knows it. But we've not said anything, you know. It's just there. And I mean, really, it's crazy. We've been out alone a handful of times, we talk on the phone, we see each other during the day when we're at the same house, but still, we've not said one word about it. And it's, well, it's because of Katherine. Drew knows she exists. Drew knows I'm not single. So maybe she's okay with us just being friends. I mean, maybe she's just content to hang out."

"And you're living in a dream world."

"So I shouldn't go out with her?"

"If you're believing this dribble that you're spewing, no. But why can't you just be honest with her?"

"Honesty is scary."

"Honesty is the best policy."

Jay laughed and went to Audrey, wrapping her arms around her. "I love you. I swear, you make sense even when you make no sense."

"I know. I'm the best friend ever."

"You are."

"Thank you. And I love you too."

CHAPTER TEN

At four thirty, her phone rang. And it wasn't the call she was expecting. It was Katherine.

"Hey."

"Well, hi, stranger."

Stranger? Jay held back her sarcastic reply and forced a smile. "Taking a break?" she asked casually.

"Just got out of a meeting. I thought I'd call since I had the chance. Where are you?"

"At one of the new houses. Just finishing up the kitchen," she said, glancing at the one painted wall.

"How's that going?"

"Good. We're done painting the first house. Just starting on the second."

"And who is *we* again?"

Jay took a deep breath, trying to pretend Katherine was interested. It was at least the third time she'd asked the question. "Connie. She's the engineering student."

"Oh, that's right. Well, I just wanted to tell you that I know it's Thursday, but I doubt I'll make it home in time for dinner. This meeting really set me back several hours."

Jay flicked her glance to the ceiling. *Surprise, surprise.* Katherine hadn't made a Thursday dinner in the last six weeks. "It's okay."

"I promise I'll make it up to you."

"Sure."

"You say that as if you don't believe me."

Jay bit her lip. She didn't want to get into it with Katherine over the phone. "Sorry. I'm sure you'll make it up to me." She paused. "And just what is it you're making up?" she asked, unable to resist.

"Jay, please don't start. I've had a very bad week. I was thinking, maybe I'll take the weekend off. How does that sound?"

"Off? Like not go to work?"

"Well, I'll have to bring work home, of course. But I thought maybe I could make a short day of it Saturday, say come home by noon. Then just work from home on Sunday. How does that sound?"

Sounds like you'll still be working. But she gave the expected answer. "Sounds great, Kath. Maybe we can have a meal together."

"Wonderful. Let's plan it, then."

The line went dead before she could reply, and Jay simply folded her phone, sliding down the wall to the floor. She closed her eyes. Was it Katherine she was angry with or herself? No matter how hard she pretended they still had a relationship, she knew it was fading fast. She suspected Katherine knew it too.

Was the current state of their relationship the result of Katherine working so much and being away, or was working an excuse so that Katherine *could* be away?

Eight years was a long time. A lot of years to throw away. Was that why they were hanging on? Pretending?

Jay's phone rang again, halting her thoughts. This time it was Drew. She felt a bit of her sadness lift.

"Hey you."

"I'm decent."

"Are you now? And clean?"

"Somewhat. They have a pool here."

"You washed in the pool?"

"I did a few laps."

Jay closed her eyes. "Wearing what?" she asked quietly.

"Wearing nothing, Jay."

She tried not to picture her naked, she really did. But she remembered the bronze torso she'd seen that first day, covered only in a red sports bra. It didn't take much imagination to lose the bra and shorts. *Sweet Jesus.* "That was mean."

"You asked."

"Soggy wet clothes would have been the appropriate answer."

Drew laughed. "My hair looks frightful. Will that help?"

"A little."

"So, still want to get together?"

"Yes," she said without hesitation.

"Meet at Rhonda's? Or want to go somewhere else?"

"No. A burger sounds good."

"Can you get away now?"

"Yes. I'm all done."

"Great. See you in a bit."

Jay again folded her phone, stretching her legs out on the floor as she leaned back against the wall, her eyes closed. Katherine brought her down. Drew lifted her up.

What a mess.

Drew waved as Jay walked in, a matching smile on her face. Jay was dressed similarly, khaki shorts and tank top tucked in, sandals on her feet. She looked cool, belying the nearly one hundred degrees outside.

"Your hair looks like it always does," Jay said.

Drew ran her fingers through it, feeling the dampness still. "I'm not sure that's a compliment."

"Of course it is." Jay pulled out a chair and sat opposite her, her eyes warm as they met Drew's.

"Would it be forward of me if I said I missed seeing you today?"

Jay smiled. "Forward, yes. But I missed you being around too."

"I suppose that's a bad thing, huh?"

"Pretty bad, yes."

"So I guess you're sorry you ran into my truck that day, right?"

"Absolutely not," Jay said with a smile. "But it does pose a problem."

"How so?"

Jay met her gaze. "Can't we have a drink first?"

Drew nodded. "On its way. I told Rhonda your usual. I wasn't sure if you had a special margarita or not." Drew watched Jay, wondering what thoughts were going through her mind this evening. Her eyes, while warm, had a wariness about them that she wasn't sure she'd seen before.

Jay leaned her elbows on the table, staring at Drew, holding her eyes. Drew couldn't look away even if she tried.

"I'm having a bit of a problem," Jay finally said.

Drew said nothing, waiting.

"Katherine and I have been together eight years. And mostly, it was a good eight years. But now, she's turned into this psychotic workaholic," she said, pulling her glance away. "For the last year, she's worked every day, every weekend. It's gotten to where we hardly see each other, hardly talk."

"No wonder you have so much free time."

"Yeah. That's where I give thanks for Audrey. She's always there when I need a pal." She paused, smiling at Shelly who brought their drinks. "You working the late shift today, Shell?"

"Margo called in sick so I'm pulling a double." She placed the margarita in front of Jay and slid the beer to Drew. "You want your usual burger, Jay?"

"Please."

"Drew? What's your fancy tonight?"

"I think I'll have the fried catfish basket."

"With two shrimp on the side?"

"If you can sneak them in."

"Like always. Coming right up."

Drew waited for Jay to sip from her drink before continuing. She had a feeling she knew where the conversation was going, but she wanted Jay to have her say.

"So anyway, I have no idea where my relationship is headed, no idea how long it'll last. And then I meet you," Jay said quietly. She looked up, meeting Drew's eyes again. "It's no secret to you, I suppose, that I'm attracted to you."

Drew shrugged. "The feeling is mutual."

"Yes, that's what I'm afraid of. That's why I don't think it's a good idea for us to see each other."

Drew attempted a smile. "You breaking up with me already?"

Jay smiled too. "I can't offer you anything, Drew. My life's a mess right now. And I need to figure out what I'm going to do. I don't want you to be a factor."

Drew leaned her arms on the table, reaching across to grasp Jay's hand. "If you think I'm waiting around for you to be single, that's just not the case. I know where I stand with you, Jay. I know what the rules are, what my limits are." She released Jay's hand. "I enjoy your company. I think you enjoy mine. I think we have the makings of a really good friendship. So please don't think I sit here undressing you with my eyes all the time. I'm not that shallow. I genuinely like you."

Jay spun her glass slowly on the table, making water rings as the ice melted. Jay finally looked at her and she fell into those blue eyes. Yes, she knew what her limits were but that didn't make it easier. She couldn't remember the last time she was so enthralled with someone.

"So you think we can be friends? Just friends?"

Drew nodded. "Yes. In fact, I have a blind date tomorrow night. Some attorney. I might get lucky."

Jay laughed. "Here's where I tell you to *run*! Never date an attorney."

"She's supposed to be very nice. It's a foursome dinner date."

"Who is she? Maybe I know her."

"Oh, I don't even know her name. We're meeting for steaks at The Pinnacle."

"And a romantic sunset over the lake?"

"Well, it'll be a sunset. I don't know how romantic it'll be." Drew paused. "What about you? Any plans for the weekend?"

Jay gave a bright smile but Drew suspected it was forced.

"Katherine plans to take it easy this weekend. Only work until noon on Saturday, then work from home on Sunday. I don't suppose I'll know what to do if I actually get to see her."

CHAPTER ELEVEN

After spending a miserable Friday trying to paint in a house whose air conditioning was not working, and where there was no sign of Drew or any of her crews, Jay gave up at two o'clock.

"Let's call it a day. I'm sweltering."

"We've been sweltering since nine this morning."

"Mr. Kline promised the AC would be working by Monday. Let's pick it up then."

"Great. I'm going home, slipping into my bikini, and hitting the pool."

Bikini. Oh, to be twenty-two again. The only time Jay braved a bikini was in her own backyard. "I'll clean up, Connie. Go jump in your pool. Have a good weekend."

"Fabulous. You do the same."

She was gone without another word, and Jay moved silently around the room, closing up paint and gathering their drop cloth. She picked up the bucket where they'd tossed the used brushes. She would clean them later with mineral spirits. Now, she just wanted to get out of the heat.

After one last check through the house, she locked up. She stood on the driveway, looking at the dirt surrounding the house, wondering why Drew hadn't shown up today.

Of course, they were probably finishing up at the other house. And then, well, Drew had a date this evening. She would probably make it an early day.

Jay sighed, hating the way she was feeling. She suspected Drew had stayed away intentionally, trying to let Jay know that she was no threat.

But she could have at least called.

Jay looked at her watch. It wouldn't hurt for *her* to call, she supposed. Just to tell her to have a good time tonight. So, after stowing all her gear and supplies in the van, she did what she abhorred in other people. She sat in the van with the motor running, AC on high, and pulled out her cell.

And after four rings, when she suspected voice mail, Drew's out-of-breath voice was heard.

"Where'd I run you from?"

"The pool."

"Again?"

"Mine this time."

Jay heard water splash. "And you're back in it?"

"It's hot as Hades today."

"Tell me. We were at the new house. No AC."

"Oh, you're kidding. I'm thankful I didn't come around then."

Jay paused. "And why was that?"

"Well, we finished up the other house this morning. And it was so hot—and a Friday—I told the guys to take off."

"Aren't you the good boss."

"What about you? Closing down early?"

"Yes. I sent Connie home. It's just too hot to work."

There was a silence on the phone, something they'd never had before. Jay leaned her head back, wondering what to say.

"Jay?"

"Hmm?"

"I stayed away on purpose, you know."

Jay nodded. "Yes, I know."

"And I really hope you guys have a good weekend. I mean that."

Jay bit her lip. "And I hope you have a great blind date tonight."

"We'll catch up next week, okay?"

"Right."

Jay tossed her phone on the seat like she always did, leaning her head back, staring at nothing. They were both lying. And they both knew it.

I hope she has a horrible time tonight.

Drew placed her phone on the flat surface of the limestone rock, then ducked back under the water. It *was* hot as Hades, but that wasn't why she was whiling away the afternoon in her pool. Truth was, she was working herself into exhaustion, trying to get Jay Burns out of her mind. She'd said all the right things last night at dinner. And at the time, she'd meant them.

But when she got home and walked into her empty house, she realized she'd been lying. Finally, after all these years, she'd met the one woman who captivated her, who held her attention, who made her laugh, who was bright and intelligent . . . and who was honest and loyal. But loyal to someone else. And honest enough to admit her feelings.

But at least they'd talked about it. At least they admitted that there was something between them. At least it was out in the open now.

Not that anything would come of it. Because they were going to be *friends*.

And so she had stayed away. They could have started on the new house, *should* have started. They'd be busting their asses next week to get it finished. But she just couldn't bring herself to see Jay, to look at her, knowing she'd lied last night. Yes, she undressed Jay with her eyes. Yes, she longed for Jay to be single and available, and no, she wasn't perfectly content being only friends with her.

So that's why, with luck, her blind date would turn out to be fantastic. Maybe so fantastic that it turned into a second date. And a second date might involve sex. And maybe, just maybe, she could get Jay out of her mind.

CHAPTER TWELVE

It wasn't that she was really counting on Katherine keeping her word, but just in case, it'd be nice to spend the afternoon by the pool, being lazy. Then later, she'd grill them each a steak, perhaps have an early dinner.

Is that what she wanted? Early dinner. Early to bed. Time to be together, perhaps even make love like they used to. Is that what she wanted?

It's what she *should* want, she realized. In reality, she knew she was simply going through the motions. She doubted she and Katherine could actually spend two days together. She wasn't sure they still knew how to talk to one another. And what in the world would they talk about? Katherine could care less about Jay's business, seemingly on the verge of flourishing finally. She'd gotten a call from another builder yesterday evening, a builder that Randy Kline had recommended her to. But Katherine wouldn't care about that. Jay's business was nothing more than a hobby, something to keep her busy while Katherine brought home the real money.

So, they would end up talking about Katherine's busy schedule, her clients, her potential, and her future. All of which was so much more important than Jay's.

She stood on the patio watching the water shimmer, the ceiling fan blowing cool air on her. She hadn't realized how bitter she'd become in the last year. Hardened and bitter. She felt her shoulders sag, felt that unnamed weight settle again.

She wanted to be happy, she wanted to enjoy her life again. She wanted to be that carefree, easygoing girl she used to be. The one who'd left Lubbock on a Greyhound bus bound for Austin, not full of regret, but full of optimism. She'd hated her life in Lubbock, hated hiding from her family, hated being the outcast. In Austin, she'd be free, she could do want she wanted, be who she wanted to be.

And in the beginning, she was. She had enough money saved that she wasn't arriving destitute. And she wasn't afraid to work. She had enough design classes and enough natural talent that Wilkes and Bonner hired her full-time after only six months. She was happy. She had income. She had an apartment. And she'd met Audrey, whom she'd become fast friends with. How she and Katherine ended up dating was still a mystery. It wasn't like they had mutual friends. They met by chance at Zilker Park one day, literally running into each other on the hike and bike trail. A coffee date turned into lunch, which led to a dinner date. Jay remembered being fascinated by Katherine, loving her aspirations, her passion for her chosen profession. She'd fallen in love with her so quickly, she didn't have a chance to see beyond the hero worship she'd developed. She moved out of her apartment and into Katherine's house, an old but spacious home in Hyde Park. They'd lived there three years before Katherine built the mansion, as Audrey called it. Now, five years of living among the rich in Austin, Jay was no closer to accepting her life here than she was when they'd moved. She *hated* the house. Oh, of course she enjoyed the amenities, like the pool, like the cleaning service that came twice a week, the yard men, the lady who picked up their laundry three times a week. All of those things were nice. Not *normal*, certainly, but nice. Because every once in a while, she enjoyed running the vacuum, she enjoyed washing and folding her own clothes, and she enjoyed keeping up the house. Because no matter how hard Katherine tried to change her, Jay was still the middle child from a hard-working middle-class family living on the outskirts of Lubbock. She would never be the socialite that Katherine was. She didn't come from money and didn't know how to spend it freely. She still saved every penny she could—for a rainy day, as her grandmother used to say—and still frowned upon extravagant purchases.

And now here she was, staring out at the crystal clear pool, a pool that was tended to twice a week by three bronzed gym rats who enjoyed parading around in nothing but their Speedos as they cleaned pool after pool here in the hills of northwest Austin.

In a fit of defiance, Jay ripped her T-shirt over her head and dropped her shorts where she stood, diving naked into the pool. She didn't care that their neighbors, with their three-story home, could see into the backyard. She didn't care that it was nearly noon, a time when Katherine said she'd be home. And she didn't care, period. She swam the length of the pool, her arms moving powerfully through the water, then kicked the wall and swam back. It felt good, the cool water, the activity. She felt the blood flowing, felt some of her earlier bitterness fade. This was her life now, the life she'd chosen, a life with Katherine. And another of her grandmother's sayings came to mind . . . *you made your bed, now lie in it.*

She stood in the shallow end, a smile turning into a laugh. She slicked her hair back and looked around. No, this certainly wasn't the life she'd chosen, not this huge house and this gorgeous pool. She sighed, her smile fading. They'd both changed, no doubt, but the woman Katherine had evolved into was nowhere near the woman she'd fallen in love with all those years ago.

But she'd made her bed . . . and this was her life now.

"For better or worse," she murmured, finally getting out of the pool and picking up her discarded clothes.

Despite the heat, Jay couldn't stand being cooped up inside her tiny office. So she hauled her laptop, her design book, and her pile of swatches out to the covered patio, turned the ceiling fans on high, and sipped on a tall glass of iced tea as she worked.

And as the clock ticked nearer to two, she'd given up on Katherine. Noon had come and gone with no sign of her, and no phone call. She wasn't surprised. Katherine had no doubt forgotten all about their plans for the weekend.

That was why, a few minutes later, her head jerked up when she heard the garage door open.

My God, she's actually home.

But the backyard door to the garage didn't open, so Jay looked for her inside, watching her walk to the double doors, standing there gazing out. She was still striking, despite being only months away from forty. Her long blond hair was thick and shiny, her features as flawless as the day they'd met. It still surprised her that some thought of them as sisters, both being blond and blue-eyed. But Katherine was always much more attractive, carrying herself with a confidence born of money and prestige, something Jay knew nothing about.

Katherine paused at the door, looking at Jay through the clear panes. She finally pushed them open and Jay noticed the smile Katherine forced to her face. She realized she was doing the same.

"What in the world are you doing outside? You must be miserable."

Jay lifted up her shirt, revealing her swimsuit. "I take a dip to cool off, then sit under the fan. It's not bad. But *you* must be miserable. A suit? On a Saturday?"

Katherine shrugged. "Habit. Let me go change. Actually, a dip in the pool sounds pretty good. I think I'll join you."

Jay watched her go, her smile turning into a frown. It was the first time she'd seen Katherine outside in the daylight in weeks. She looked tired. Her eyes were nearly lifeless. Jay shook her head. No one could exist on four hours sleep a day indefinitely. Apparently, it had caught up with Katherine.

She set her laptop aside and followed Katherine into the house. "You want something to drink?" she called up the stairs. "I have a pitcher of tea."

"I'd prefer something stronger. Something cool for outside. How about a Tom Collins?"

"Sure." *Gin? At this hour?*

Jay went to the bar, finding the gin and Tom Collins mix. She sliced up a lime and stuck that on the side of the glass, then took a lime wedge and added it to her iced tea. She took both drinks outside and waited for Katherine to return.

And when she did, standing there in her swimsuit, Jay's eyebrows shot up.

"My God, how much weight have you lost?" she blurted out without thinking. Katherine looked nearly gaunt.

"I know. I haven't been eating. Stress."

"How much longer can you keep this up, Kath? You're killing yourself."

She flashed a charming smile. "Hardly killing myself. But it won't be much longer."

"Is making partner worth all this?"

"Partner? Oh, that's in the bag, sweetheart. Has been. But in another month, I will have brought in more clients and more money than anyone *ever* has in the history of the firm. Old man

Mills about has a coronary each week when he looks at the numbers. I love it."

With that, she dove into the pool, swimming underwater until she reached the other side, then floated on her back as she kicked her legs lazily.

"And after I've sucked all his clients from him, I'm going to start my own firm. Won't that be great?"

"Wonderful," Jay said, trying to muster up some enthusiasm.

"Oh, I forgot to tell you who I ran into yesterday at lunch. Do you remember me telling you about that girl I met in law school? Jenna White?"

Jay nodded. "Your first, right? She ended up being straight?"

Katherine laughed. "She *wanted* to be straight, yes. Anyway, I saw her at Juan's yesterday during lunch. She's been back in town for five months already. I can't believe I haven't run into her before now."

"Really?" *Lunch? She takes time for lunch?* "What's she doing back?"

"She's divorced. Seems being straight didn't work out for her," Katherine said with a laugh. "She's working at Bateman."

"What a coincidence."

"Yes, I thought so." Katherine swam closer. "We're going to hook up next week for lunch one day to catch up. I thought it'd be nice to maybe have her over for dinner one night. Would you mind cooking?"

"Of course not. But will you be joining us?"

"Very funny. Of course I'll be joining you. I'll just have to make it a point to leave work early."

Jay wasn't sure if her sudden burst of anger was based on jealously or not. But really, did Katherine even hear what she was saying? She meets her at lunch, yet can't ever break away when Jay suggests they meet for a quick bite. And dinner? When was the last time Katherine *made it a point* to get home early for dinner? No, she was just too busy to make time for Jay. But for an old girlfriend? Sure, no problem.

"It's funny, really," Katherine said as she splashed around in the water. "In law school, she would have just *died* had anyone said she was gay. You should see her now. She's all *out there*, you know. She said being married opened her eyes. She couldn't stand having to answer to a man." Katherine laughed. "Now she's working for Bateman. Talk about a control freak. She won't last there the year."

"Well, if you start your own firm, perhaps you can bring her on board," Jay said lightly.

"I've already thought of that. Of course, just because she's an old friend won't hold much weight if she doesn't have the clients." Katherine flipped over to her back. "Why don't you come join me?"

Jay hesitated, wanting to decline. But really, when was the last time they'd had a Saturday afternoon together? "Sure."

"What do you have planned for dinner?"

Jay dove into the pool, surfacing several feet from Katherine. "I thought we'd grill steaks out here. It's been awhile."

"Sounds good. And I wouldn't mind an early dinner. I'm exhausted, really. This was a good idea to have a short weekend for once."

"Yes, it was. And forgive me for saying so, but Kath, you look terrible."

Katherine laughed. "Thanks, sweetheart."

"I mean it. You look like you could just collapse. I'm not sure you can go another month like this."

"I have to. And it won't be a problem. When they announce my new position, I'll be able to take some time off." She stood in the pool, wringing her long hair behind her. "I thought maybe we could get away somewhere." She looked over at Jay. "How about Hawaii?"

"*Hawaii?*"

"You've never been, have you?"

Jay just barely resisted rolling her eyes. Of course she'd never been. Katherine knew that. "No, I've not had the pleasure."

"Well, then maybe we'll think about doing that. My treat, of course." She walked out of the pool and plopped down in one of the lounge chairs in the shade. "You were right. It's quite pleasant out here after a swim."

"Yes, it is," Jay replied before ducking under the water again and swimming to the far end. *Hawaii?* Good Lord, what had gotten into her?

Katherine covered her mouth as another yawn came over her. "I'm sorry. I guess I'm not used to down time."

"Maybe your body is trying to tell you something."

Katherine sipped from her fourth Tom Collins of the afternoon. "It's telling me I'm starving. Those steaks smell wonderful."

"And they'll be ready in a second. Do you want to eat out here or inside?"

"Oh, we're still in our swimsuits. Let's stay out."

"Okay. Let me get the asparagus and potatoes, I'll be right back." Jay hurried inside, ignoring the table she'd already set for dinner. She stood on tiptoe, trying to reach the large serving platter and failing.

"Crap," she muttered. She got the small step stool from the utility room, pulling down the stainless steel platter which they seldom used. On it, she placed two plates and utensils, cloth napkins, the bowl of potatoes and the steamed asparagus. She hurried back outside, kicking open the door with her foot, scowling at the smoke coming from the grill. "Kath, turn the steaks," she said.

Katherine lifted the lid, ducking back from the smoke before flipping their rib eyes over. She looked at Jay over the rim of the gas grill. "Were we out of filet mignon?"

"Sorry. You'll have to settle for rib eye."

"You should make a note to stock up," she said. "I much prefer them."

Jay bit her lip as she set the table outside. "Of course, Kath. But these are prime cut." She walked over to the grill. "And they're ready to come off." She took the tongs from Katherine. "Go sit. I'll bring them over."

Katherine took her drink and moved away. She stood looking out over the pool, finally turning back to Jay. "You're very good to me, you know."

"You think?"

"Yes. I haven't been very good to you this past year."

Jay hesitated, torn between agreeing with her and perhaps having that discussion Audrey had urged her to have . . . or simply ignoring the statement and having dinner. She met Katherine's eyes, still so lifeless. She chose to ignore it. "You've been very busy, Kath, I know that. And I've been busy with my business. It's starting to take off, I think."

Katherine nodded, but didn't comment.

"Sit. Make yourself a plate. Do you want another drink?"

"No, I think I've had enough." She sat down. "But where's my steak sauce?"

"Sorry. I forgot it. Be right back." Jay hurried back into the house, nearly exhausted herself, just from serving dinner. She stopped in the kitchen, taking a breath. Had it always been this way? Had she always been the caretaker? Had Katherine always been the queen?

Yes.

And without warning, that heavy weight settled around her again, making her shoulders ache, making her chest heavy. A feeling of confinement, of imprisonment, washed over her, making her breath hard to catch, her lungs tight. She leaned against the counter, eyes closed, trying to ward off the dizziness.

Anxiety attack?

73

But it passed as soon as it started, her head clearing, the ache leaving her shoulders. "Christ," she murmured, rubbing the back of her neck.

"Jay?"

Jay turned, expecting Katherine to be standing there. But she was still on the patio. "Coming." She found Katherine's favorite steak sauce in the fridge and hurried back outside.

"The seasoning is great on these. I almost don't need the sauce."

Jay gritted her teeth and placed the steak sauce within Katherine's reach. "Well, just in case."

CHAPTER THIRTEEN

Jay stomped across the drop cloth, her mood still as sour as it had been on Sunday. And if she'd had a can of paint opened, she very well might have flung it against the wall.

"What is wrong with you?"

Jay glanced at Connie. "Nothing."

"I think you should let me do the painting today. You're in some kind of mood."

Jay whipped around, angry. But Connie simply stood there, a concerned look on her face. "God, I'm sorry," Jay said. "I really am."

"Bad weekend?"

"Yeah."

"Relationship hell?"

Jay laughed. "Something like that. But I think you're right. I should let you work. I'll make a run to the paint store. Get what

I need for the bedroom. How does that sound?"

Connie waved her away. "Take your time. The AC is working today. I'll be fine."

Jay left without another word, going through the front door and standing on the stoop, looking out over the yard, watching as Drew's guy Johnny gave instructions to the five young men with him.

"Hey," she called, waiting until Johnny turned around. "Where's Drew?"

Johnny shook his head. "She won't be out until this afternoon. Had a meeting with a builder this morning."

Jay nodded. Okay, at least Drew wasn't still avoiding her. She jogged down the sidewalk to her van, starting the engine and turning the AC on high. She sat there, hands gripped tightly on the steering wheel. *Yeah, relationship hell.*

Katherine had made it about halfway through dinner before exhaustion—and alcohol—claimed her. She practically had to be carried up the stairs to bed. And at midnight, when Jay had ventured into their bedroom, Katherine woke, wanting to make love. Jay had given in to the familiar touch, trying in vain to conjure up those old feelings. Katherine's kisses were soft, gentle . . . like she remembered. Her touch was light across her skin. But that was all. There was no passion, no urgency in their embrace. And before either of them had even come close to orgasm, Katherine had fallen asleep again, forgetting all about their lovemaking, stopping in mid-stroke and rolling over to face the wall.

Jay had never been more humiliated in all her life. She withdrew her fingers from Katherine and slipped from the bed, going back outside to sit by the pool. It was hours later before sleep claimed her.

And the next morning, Katherine had cuddled with her in bed, whispering how wonderful the sex had been the night before. Thankfully, Katherine was invigorated and had practically run down the stairs and into her office, working the morning away until Jay had called her for lunch. A lunch Katherine only picked at before dashing away to the firm, saying she had files she *had* to work on.

And when Jay awoke at two the next morning, Katherine had been sleeping beside her. And at six, Katherine had been gone.

She sighed. So much for their weekend together.

She pulled away from the curb, her tires squealing. And yes, she was in some kind of mood.

Drew stepped out of her truck, disappointed that Jay's van was nowhere in sight. She slammed her door, squinting into the sun as she watched Johnny and his crew unload grass pallets from the trailer.

"About time you show up," Johnny called.

Drew pointed at her clothes. "Don't think I'll be helping you today."

"So you just stopped by to supervise then, huh?"

"Of course."

"And I know you're lying. You just missed her." He pointed down the street. "She went that way. Was in a bit of a hurry too. Left tire marks."

Drew looked at the street, seeing the faint mark of tire treads. She nodded. "Be right back."

She went to the door and knocked once, then went inside. She found Connie on the floor in the living room, her head bobbing to a silent beat. Drew frowned, then noticed the white wires going to each ear. She walked closer, then nudged Connie with her foot. The girl nearly jumped out of her skin.

"Jesus Christ!" she yelled, ripping both wires from her ears. She touched her chest. "Christ, Drew, you nearly killed me."

"Sorry, kid. Where's Jay?"

"She left."

"So I heard. What's up?"

"I don't know, but she's in some kind of mood. She had a bad weekend or something."

Drew raised her eyebrows. "Where'd she go?"

"She went to the paint store. Shopping cures all ails, you know."

"Does it now?"

"Well, for most women," she said. "You may not fit into that category."

Drew laughed. "I think I'll take that as a compliment." Drew turned away and pulled out her phone, dialing Jay.

"Hey."

"Hey, yourself," Drew said as she moved back outside. "Where are you?"

"At the paint store, arguing with Tim over color mixes."

"I see. Is everything okay?"

"Of course." Then she paused and Drew waited. "Not really, no."

"Wanna talk about it?" She heard the sigh, felt the hesitation.

"I'm okay, Drew. Just had a bad weekend. You know, Katherine and I aren't used to spending time together. And it didn't go so well."

"Okay. I was just checking on you. Johnny said you left tire treads when you pulled away and Connie said you were—"

"In some kind of mood," Jay finished for her. "I know." Another pause. "How was your weekend?"

"Not bad. Okay."

"You had a date Friday night. How was that?"

It was Drew's turn to hesitate. She looked up into the clear sky, trying to form the words. *How was it?* Well, it was okay as far as blind dates went. And she liked her well enough. It's just, well, there wasn't that spark, that interest. And she didn't have blue eyes that captivated her. They were neutral brown. So how was it? "It was better than some," she finally said. "Not too bad."

"Great." Another pause. "Are you going to see her again?"

Drew smiled at Jay's attempt at showing polite interest, all the while fishing for information. "Yes, I'll probably see her again."

"Wonderful."

"Yeah."

"Good."

"Uh-huh."

"I should go," Jay said quickly. "Tim is glaring at me."

"Okay."

"Will you be at the house?"

"No. I'm not dressed for work. Had a meeting."

"So I heard. Then I guess I won't see you."

"I'll be around tomorrow, Jay."

As soon as she hung up with Drew, Jay smiled apologetically at Tim, then turned her back to him, dialing Audrey's office. She paced, waiting for her to answer.

"You called the secret hotline. Something must be up."

Jay smiled. "Hey. Sorry to bother you at work, but I need you."

"No problem. What's up?"

"I need a therapy session. Can you do lunch?"

"Lunch? Must be serious."

Jay bit her lip. "Audrey, I think I'm losing my mind."

Audrey laughed. "You're just now realizing that, huh?"

"I'm serious. My life is a total mess. I had an awful weekend, just awful. And now Drew is avoiding me, I know she is. Just because, you know, we had *the talk* last week."

"The *talk*?"

"You know, the I'm attracted to you talk, but there's Katherine."

"Oh, *that* talk. Okay, let's do lunch. Meet you there at one?"

"Thanks, pal."

◈◈◈

"So she actually fell asleep during sex?"

Jay blushed. "Yes. I mean, right smack in the middle of it, then couldn't remember it the next morning. How sad is that?"

"Let's get back to this Hawaii thing. That sounds like fun."

"That's another thing. She wants to get away for a couple of weeks. *Hawaii?* We couldn't spend one weekend together. How the hell are we supposed to spend two weeks?"

"I think she realizes how far you've drifted apart. Maybe this is her way of trying to get you back on track. And Hawaii, well, you'll both be removed from your work and friends, it'll just be the two of you. This could be the either sink or swim part of your relationship. After two weeks together, you'll know whether you should try to salvage it or just let it go."

"Oh, and I didn't tell you this. She met an old friend of hers at lunch one day last week. *At lunch.* I didn't think she ever took a lunch because every time I offer, she's too busy. But that's another issue. Anyway, this friend—an old girlfriend—they're going to do lunch this week to catch up, and she thought it'd be nice if we invited her over to dinner. I'll cook, of course. And Katherine will *make it a point* to get home early that evening to entertain. Can you believe that? And she had no clue how hurtful that was to me. I was floored. I mean, I don't think she did it on purpose. Surely she wouldn't do it intentionally. But it hurts to know she'll make time for someone else, but doesn't make the effort with me."

"I agree, that is cruel. But she's just not thinking. You know what they say, you always take the one closest to you for granted."

Jay rubbed her temples. "Part of me feels like a spoiled brat, wanting attention, you know. Like a *pathetic* spoiled brat, I might add."

"Oh, don't be silly. Anyone would be pissed off."

Jay looked up. "Audrey, how did it get like this? Two years ago, I was happy, wasn't I?"

"You were . . . content, I think. That's a better word. I don't know that I'd use the happy word."

"Of course I was happy. We still saw each other, we still did things together." She tilted her head. "Didn't we?"

"Let's see, two years ago, she took that trip to New Zealand with a friend because you couldn't get away for three weeks. Remember?"

"Well, yeah, but that wasn't her fault."

"And wasn't it around that time you started complaining that the only time you went out was with friends of hers? That the two of you never took the time to go out alone?"

"Jesus, Audrey, what'd you do? Store away information for later use?"

"Hey, you asked."

"So you think after eight years Katherine is tired of my company?"

"I think after eight years, the shortcomings of your relationship have become more glaring, that's all. The newness is gone. The need to please has subsided. Differences now become more apparent."

Jay leaned forward. "So exactly how many psychology classes did you take in college?"

"Oh, Jay, when two people quit working at a relationship, this is what happens. Doesn't take a degree in psychology to figure it out."

"I don't think I've quit working at it," Jay protested.

Audrey stared at her. "Can you honestly say you're still in love with her?"

Jay opened her mouth to say just that, then closed it again. *Was she?* After eight years, love evolves, feelings change . . . emotions shift. Was she still in love with Katherine? She finally dared to meet Audrey's eyes. "I don't think I am," she whispered.

Audrey reached across the table and squeezed her hand. "Which brings us to Drew."

Jay slowly shook her head. "I can't deal with Drew right now. I think it was too ambitious of me to try to be friends with her. I . . . I get around her and I just lose all sense, you know."

"That's because you're attracted to her."

"Well, I can't be attracted to her right now." Jay rubbed her temples again. "Do you think I should talk to Katherine about this? Do you think we should have a heart-to-heart?"

Audrey grinned. "I'd wait until after the Hawaii trip."

CHAPTER FOURTEEN

"So, are you avoiding me or am I avoiding you?" Drew asked after she'd cornered Jay in the kitchen.

"I don't know what you mean."

Drew raised an eyebrow. "Well, I'd thought I was the one keeping my distance, but now I'm not so sure."

Jay leaned against the counter, wondering if Connie could hear their conversation, and wondering why she even cared. "I'm not really avoiding you, no."

"Not really?"

Jay pointed her finger at Drew. "But you can't say the same, can you?"

Drew took a step closer. "Look, I just thought, after our little talk, that you'd be more comfortable if you didn't see me every single day."

"So you *were* avoiding me," Jay said.

"Perhaps."

"And you've been out three times now with your blind date?"

"Yes."

"So what does that mean? Now you're going to break up with me?"

Drew laughed. "Cute."

Jay smiled. "Yeah, thought so."

Drew moved farther into the kitchen, standing close to Jay. "What are we going to do?"

"We can't do anything, Drew. Nothing's changed."

Drew caught Jay's eyes, seeing the sadness there, wondering if it were for her. She tilted her head. "What's wrong?" she asked quietly.

Jay looked away. "My life's a mess."

"Why do you say that?"

"Because I don't know what's happening with it any longer, that's why. Katherine and I are strangers, really. The woman I've lived with for eight years has turned into someone I don't even know." She looked up. "And you, Jesus, you confuse the hell out of me."

"Me?"

"Yeah, you. I feel things when I'm around you." She met her eyes again. "Things I haven't felt in a very long time," she said softly. "And it scares me."

"Don't let it scare you, Jay. I told you, I know where I stand with you."

"I don't even know where you stand with me. How can you?"

"Look, whatever you're going through with Katherine, that's between you two. I'm just doing my thing, okay? I don't want to complicate anything for you. Right now, we're just friends. That's it. Whatever feelings are there, they're just going to be there. We'll work around them."

Jay shook her head. "I'm insanely jealous that you're on a third date with someone."

Drew leaned closer, her face only inches from Jay's. "And I'm insanely jealous that someone's had eight years with you."

CHAPTER FIFTEEN

"Dinner? *Tomorrow* night?" Jay asked, holding her paintbrush in one hand and cell in the other.

"Yes. That won't be a problem, will it?"

"I just wish you'd given me a little more warning. I've got work planned all day tomorrow. Now I have to squeeze in shopping and cooking."

Katherine laughed. "How hard can that be?"

"A meal just doesn't miraculously appear on the table, Kath. And I have a deadline here, you know." Jay looked around her, the stained drop cloth littered with her painting supplies.

"Then let's just cater dinner and be done with it. Call a restaurant and order something extravagant. We could do French."

"No, that's ridiculous. I can manage."

"Then why don't you make that lovely pot roast I like? Maybe steam some asparagus? That would dress things up."

"Sure." A pot roast only took *hours*.

"Oh, and Jenna's bringing a date. I thought that would be better than just the three of us. Jenna and I will most likely sneak off to my office. I'm sure you'd be bored to tears listening to our stories."

"Of course. No problem," she said lightly. *Just how I wanted to spend my evening . . . entertaining a stranger.*

"Thanks, Jay. And since I'm making an early day of it tomorrow, I'll probably be here until after midnight. Don't wait up."

Jay nearly laughed. *Wait up?* She hadn't stayed up waiting for her in more months than she could count. In fact, there were times when she wondered if Katherine came home at all. She wasn't in bed with her when she went to sleep and she wasn't there when she woke.

And she was well past worrying about it.

CHAPTER SIXTEEN

"You have no idea how much I'm dreading this," Jay said as she walked back into her office and shut the door. "I'd rather have a root canal."

Audrey laughed. "That's because you enjoy the gas he gives you."

"You know what I mean." She plopped down into her recliner. "And with my luck, Katherine won't even make it home in time and I'll be stuck here with them."

"Oh, she'll be home in time. This is her dinner, not yours. She'll be there."

Jay glanced at her watch. "I should get in the shower. I have to prepare the salad still."

"And for dessert?"

"Shut up, Audrey."

"Oh, I know you have something planned. What is it?"

"I got apple pies at the bakery."

"And ice cream?"

"Yes, and ice cream."

"You're such a good little housewife," Audrey said. "Now go get ready. You want to make a good impression on Katherine's new friend."

"Do I?"

"Of course you do."

"Would it be uncouth to wear shorts to dinner?"

"You will not wear shorts to dinner. Wear something light. Wear slacks and a sleeveless blouse."

"Khakis and sandals?"

"You can't wear your Teva sandals to a nice dinner. I swear, were you raised in a barn?"

"Very funny. Okay, I'm going to go now. Wish me luck."

"I shall think of you all evening."

"You will not. I know you're going out. And remember, don't have sex with strangers." She smiled, hearing Audrey howl with laughter as she disconnected.

But her smile soon faded as the hour approached. She wasn't sure why she was dreading the evening so much. Maybe she was just apprehensive about meeting Katherine's old fling. Although to hear Katherine tell it, their affair lasted only a semester. But still, here the woman was, newly divorced and *out there*, as Katherine had said. Was she jealous? With the fragile state of their relationship, did she view Jenna as a threat? Perhaps.

Or perhaps it was just the idea she was having to put on a dinner party for two people she'd never met before.

"Smells wonderful, Jay." Katherine closed the oven door and smiled, walking closer. "You look nice."

Jay shrugged. "Thanks." A light blue silk blouse—a gift from

Katherine—and her favorite khaki slacks won out. But she'd taken Audrey's advice on the sandals. She wore comfortable leather slip-ons instead.

"Well, let me shower and put on something a little more comfortable. Why don't you put some music on? Jazz perhaps? Jenna used to love jazz."

Jay nodded. "Sure." *She knows I hate jazz.*

"Have you picked out a wine?" Katherine called from the top of the stairs. "How about that burgundy I brought back from California last year?"

"Sounds good." Although far too dry for her liking. She would force down a glass, then open another bottle on the pretense she would let Katherine and Jenna finish the very expensive bottle from California. She much preferred the German wines from that little vineyard in Bryan. "Nothing wrong with Texas wines," she muttered as she found the bottle Katherine had requested.

"Is our bar stocked?" Katherine called again from upstairs. "It's been so long since we've entertained."

Jay stood, closing the cabinet door to the hidden wine rack and opening the bar instead. It was well stocked. As Katherine said, they rarely entertained any longer. Gin, vodka, rum, bourbon and of course, her tequila, along with all the mixers to make nearly any drink. "We have plenty." In fact . . . why not start now? She was much more likely to make it through the evening with alcohol than without. So, she filled a glass with ice, poured a generous amount of gin, and topped it off with Tom Collins mix.

She took a sip, enjoying the freshness of the drink. Maybe it wouldn't be so bad. She'd had Katherine's friends over before. She'd survived.

"Did you forget about the music?"

Jay turned around, finding Katherine at the entertainment center, picking through the CDs. "Sorry." She took another sip.

"Want a drink?"

Katherine flicked her gaze at Jay. "Starting early, aren't you?"

Jay shrugged. "Had a busy, rushed day, getting Connie started at the new house, then shopping for dinner, then back at the new house." She pointed toward the kitchen. "Then back here to cook. It's been a long day already."

Katherine laughed. "Sweetheart, you don't know what a long day is. When you're at the office until midnight and only come home to catch a few hours sleep, then we'll talk."

Jay smiled humorlessly. "Of course. I forgot. You're the queen of long days. I'm actually quite shocked you were able to get away today," she said, unable to keep the sarcasm out of her voice. Fortunately—or perhaps unfortunately—Katherine didn't seem to notice.

"Well, it's not every day I run into an old friend, Jay. Of course I made it a point to be here."

Jay's eyebrows shot up but she withheld her comment, sipping from her drink instead.

"And I think I will have a drink," Katherine said after glancing at her watch. "They should be here any minute." She put several CDs in and adjusted the volume. Soon, smooth . . . and loud jazz wafted throughout the house.

And it wasn't that Jay despised jazz. Not really. It's just she liked it in small doses. *Quiet* doses. But Katherine liked it *loud*. And for some reason, Jay couldn't wrap her brain around *smooth* and *loud* jazz at the same time, even when Katherine insisted it was. "It's a bit loud for conversation," she said, trying to be heard over the music.

"You can't hear all the detail if you keep it low."

"And we won't be able to hear our company talk if you keep it loud."

Katherine only smiled and headed to the bar. "Can I get you another?"

Jay shook her head, ignoring Katherine's stare as she turned the volume down. "I refuse to entertain guests and compete with this noise at the same time."

"Noise?"

"Yes, noise. It was deafening. I'm fairly certain jazz was meant to be listened to in more subtle decibels."

"As if you know jazz," Katherine countered.

The ensuing argument was thankfully halted by the ringing of the doorbell. Katherine's eyes brightened, and she put her glass down and hurried to the door. "Wonderful. She's here."

"Wonderful," Jay mimicked.

But when Katherine opened the door, Jay's breath left her and she very nearly dropped her glass.

"Jenna, welcome," Katherine gushed. "I see you didn't have trouble finding it."

"Not at all. Of course, having a GPS system takes all the fun out of it," she said with a laugh. "And I'd like you to meet my friend, Drew Montgomery. Drew, this is Katherine, an old college friend."

Jay watched, her eyes wide as Drew—decked out in tan slacks and a dark green polo shirt—shook hands with a laughing Katherine. "What do you mean *old* college friend?" She stood rooted to the spot, her eyes darting between Drew and Katherine. Finally, Drew looked her way, her expression—Jay imagined—mirrored her own. Shock.

"Oh, here, please come in," Katherine offered, standing aside. She glanced at Jay, motioning her closer. "Jay, come meet Jenna and Drew."

Jay tried to be polite and pulled her glance from Drew, smiling quickly at Jenna before locking once again on Drew. What in the *hell* was she doing here? To her credit, Drew seemed to have recovered quite nicely.

"Nice to meet you, Jay," she said, hand outstretched. "I'm Drew Montgomery."

Her eyes twinkled and her mouth just hinted at a smile, and

Jay took her hand dumbly, acknowledging the hard squeeze Drew gave her with one of her own. "Hi, Drew," she said, pulling her hand away and offering it to Jenna. "Nice to meet you, Jenna. Katherine's told me a little about you. It's so neat that you two met up again."

"Nice to meet you too, Jay. Thanks for having us."

Jay was saved from commenting when Katherine linked arms with Jenna and led her into the house. Whereas Katherine was tall, blond . . . Jenna was short and dark-headed. And as they headed to the bar, Jay whipped her head around, glaring at Drew.

"What the *hell*?" she hissed.

Drew grinned. "Imagine *my* surprise."

"The blind date?"

"The same."

"Oh, good Lord. What are the chances?"

"Drew? Can I get you a drink?" Katherine asked from the bar.

Drew gave Jay a subtle wink. "Beer?"

Katherine looked at Jay. "Oh, my. Do we even have any?"

Jay shook her head. "No beer. Sorry." She glanced at Drew and smiled. "But we have the fixings for just about anything else."

Drew's lips twitched in amusement. "How about something fruity, then?"

Jay met her eyes, smiling in return as she remembered Drew's earlier admission that she had a fondness for fruity drinks. "Daiquiri?"

"Perfect."

"Oh, well I'll let you take care of that one, Jay," Katherine said. "I'm going to show Jenna my office real quick. You two get acquainted."

"No problem," Drew replied.

As soon as the two women walked away, Jay and Drew faced

each other, smiles turning to grins, and finally to quiet laughter.

"I cannot *believe* you're at my house for dinner. How did we not know this?"

"Well, remember, I've been avoiding you."

"Oh, that's right. You were breaking up with me."

"Do you have fresh strawberries?"

"You'll have to settle for frozen." Jay glanced over her shoulder, making sure they were still alone. "So *this* is your blind date," she stated as she pulled out the blender and filled it with ice. "And this makes what? Your fourth time out? Is it getting serious?"

"Are you asking if we've slept together?"

Jay blushed. "Of course not!" She turned the blender on, crushing the ice, then stopped. "Have you?"

Drew tilted her head, watching Jay. "Other than a few steamy goodnight kisses, no, no sex." Drew raised her eyebrows. "Which is surprising, I'll admit."

"Well, maybe she just doesn't do it for you."

"I was thinking it was the other way around. She doesn't seem to be in any hurry." Drew shrugged. "Besides, we don't really go together. We have nothing in common. And she doesn't really meet many of those qualities I'm looking for," she said with a wink. "Which is why it's surprising we've been out four times. And there's not even any sex going on."

"You never did tell me what all those qualities were, you know," Jay said as she added frozen strawberries to her mixture before turning on the blender again.

Drew waited until the blender finished before answering. She held up a hand, ticking off each finger. "Honest, funny, loyal, talented, beautiful, *single*," she added with emphasis. "And of course be madly in love with me."

"That's all, huh?"

"What? Too ambitious?"

Jay poured Drew's drink and handed it to her. "Try this."

Drew took a sip, nodding. "Excellent."

"Good. And no, not too ambitious. Everyone should have standards." Jay filled her own glass with ice and reached for the gin. "But are you looking for someone with all of those? Or maybe just four or five?"

"Yes, all."

Jay laughed. "No wonder you're still single."

"I don't think it's that unattainable. You, for instance, meet all but two of them," Drew said seriously.

"Two?"

"Yes. You have all the qualities except two. You're not single and you're not madly in love with me," she said quietly.

Jay met her eyes, letting herself be pulled into the dark green depths. No, she wasn't single. But Lord, if she let herself, Drew would be so easy to fall in love with. She finally pulled away. "I like you . . . a lot, Drew," she said softly.

Drew sighed, a heavy sigh that caused Jay to look back at her.

"Maybe we should rethink this friendship thing," she suggested. "It's harder than I thought."

But Jay shook her head. "You're one of the very few bright spots in my life right now. Don't you dare disappear on me."

Drew held her gaze for a moment longer, then gave a slight smile. "Okay." She held her glass up. "After all, you do make a killer daiquiri."

"Wait until you taste my pot roast."

"Oh? Should I add cooking to my list, you think?"

Jay nudged her arm. "Want me to show you around?"

"Do you suppose we should find out what they're up to?" she asked, motioning to the closed door Katherine and Jenna had disappeared behind.

"I don't really care." Jay looked intently at Drew. "Do you?"

"No. So how about we start outside then?" She looked around the large living area. "No offense, but it seems kinda sterile."

Jay stifled her laugh. "Really? You'd dare say that about the *mansion?*" At Drew's confused look, Jay took her arm and led her out to the patio. "Audrey refers to it as the mansion. She *hates* it here."

"Well, I'm just surprised by it. It doesn't have your personality at all."

"*Me?*" Jay shook her head. "Oh, no. I didn't design or decorate *anything* here."

Drew frowned. "You didn't? Why?"

Jay bit her lower lip, surprised that it still stung. She *was* a designer, after all. But she tried to be diplomatic about it. "Katherine and I have different tastes."

Drew raised her eyebrows, but said nothing.

"*Very* different tastes," Jay added. At Drew's amused look, she laughed. "Oh, hell, you know what I mean." She looked back toward the double doors leading inside. "It's all so over the top for me. Even though I'm far removed from it, I'm still just a girl from a middle-class family in a small, conservative city. And this, well, this *reeks* of money. Wasted money, I might add." She turned back to the patio. "I enjoy the pool, of course. But still, it's not something I would have designed. You're right. It's sterile. It lacks feeling."

"That's a good way to put it. But I'm still surprised you weren't a part of the planning. That is your profession. I mean, it'd be like me buying one of these new houses and getting Apollo to do the yard."

"Okay, I'll admit I was totally pissed off at the time. This monster was everything she wanted and nothing for me. So our arrangement was she would pay the mortgage. And if she paid the mortgage, then she got to decorate. So she hired Wilkes and Bonner, but I wasn't allowed to participate."

"That's just wrong."

"Yes. My coworkers at Wilkes and Bonner were quite amused by it all." Jay stared again at the house. "And not that I'm dying for their company, but isn't it a bit odd that they only said a handful of words and then disappeared into her study?" She glanced at her watch. "Do you think I—"

But the doors opened, interrupting her. Katherine stood in the doorway, Jenna beside her.

"There you two are. I was wondering where you'd gone off to." She motioned back inside. "I was about to give Jenna a tour. Drew, are you interested?"

Jay saw Drew's hesitation, then watched as she nodded.

"Sure." She glanced at Jay. "Are you going to tag along?"

"Actually, I think I'll check on dinner. You all go ahead."

And as the doors closed, leaving Jay alone, she turned toward the pool, absently watching the water shimmer in the early evening light. *Damn, how weird is this?* Drew is dating Katherine's old flame. Dating, but not sleeping with. She didn't know why, but that news was pleasing to her. Not that it mattered who Drew slept with. Not that it's any of your concern, she told herself. But really, they didn't go together at all. Jenna was short . . . and not heavy, but certainly not thin. She seemed far too serious for Drew. Not that you could get a good read on a person after only exchanging greetings. But still, not her type.

And good Lord, Jenna and *Katherine*? Of course, who knew how they were all those years ago in law school. But now, no. No way.

Drew pushed her plate away, her eyes finding Jay's across the table. "That was absolutely delicious. I'm stuffed."

"Thanks. But I hope you saved room for dessert."

"I have to agree, Jay," Jenna said. "I can't remember when I've had better pot roast."

"It's my favorite meal," Katherine chimed in. "But I *did* save room for dessert. Apple pie with ice cream?" she asked, looking at Jay.

Jay nodded. "I'll bring it right out."

Drew was about to offer to help, but Jay had already hurried from the table. She glanced to her right, surprised to find Jenna blatantly staring at Katherine. She frowned, wondering at the extent of their relationship. Jenna had simply said old friends, but there was something intimate in their looks.

"After dessert, Jenna, you'll have to come into my study. I forgot to show you my collection of law books. Some date back two hundred years."

"Oh, I'd love to see them."

Katherine turned to Drew. "You'd be bored silly, dear, but you're welcome to view them too."

Drew smiled, but took the hint. "Maybe I'll get Jay to show me her portfolio. We're sort of in the same business."

"Oh, really? Jenna said you did yards. I assumed mowing and the like."

Drew laughed. "We do that too. But we're a landscaping service. I work with builders designing new homes."

"Well, I'm surprised you and Jay haven't run into each other before."

'Yeah, that is kinda weird." Drew looked up as Jay carried a tray laden with four plates and a large bowl of ice cream.

"What's weird?" Jay asked, setting the tray on the table. She handed the first piece of pie to Katherine.

"That you and I haven't run into each other before." Drew took the plate Jay handed her. "Thank you."

"Well, I've seen your trucks around. Does that count?"

Drew noticed the slight smile around Jay's mouth. "I'm not really on site all that much anyway."

"Don't do a lot of grunt work anymore?"

"As little as possible."

"Who else wants ice cream?" Katherine asked as she held up the bowl.

"None for me, thanks," Jenna said. "Goes right to my hips."

"Then I'll have your share," Drew said, reaching for the bowl. "This pie looks great."

"I can't take credit," Jay said. "It's from Dora's Bakery."

"Then I know it'll be good. I usually get my breakfast there." She passed the bowl of ice cream to Jay. "Have you had her breakfast pastries stuffed with scrambled eggs and sausage?"

"The ones with all that cheese melted on top?" Jay laughed. "I'm surprised I haven't run into you there as well."

Katherine slid her plate away from her, her pie only half eaten. "While the two of you chat about pastries and such, I'm going to show Jenna my law book collection." She stood, motioning for Jenna to join her.

Drew watched them go, then looked back to Jay. Jay met her eyes with a shrug.

"I'd rather chat about pastries and such," she said, mimicking Katherine.

Drew took a bite of pie, the melted ice cream oozing off the top. "Mmm, I'd rather eat pie."

"It's sinfully good, isn't it?"

Drew nodded. "And not that I'm prying or anything, but you and Katherine, you don't talk much, do you." It was intended to be a question, but she knew her tone indicated it was simply an observation.

"We don't talk much, we hardly see each other, and . . . and as a treat, she wants to take a two-week trip to Hawaii." Jay rested her chin in the palm of her hand. "Sometimes I feel like we're strangers, not two people in a multi-year relationship."

"People change. I'm sure you both have."

"Yes, we both have, I suppose. There's added stress in my life, trying to get my business going. There's pressure in her job, and goals she's set for herself that require an insane amount of her time. Time that we used to have together."

Drew looked at the two empty chairs at the table and the plates of half-eaten pie. "They seem to know each other well.

Jenna said they were old friends from college."

"Old friends, yes. Lovers too."

"You're kidding."

"They had an affair one semester, then Jenna decided she wasn't gay after all." Jay made a face. "Likely story."

Drew laughed. "Yeah. The Jenna I know is very comfortable with her sexuality." Drew looked around the formal dining room, shaking her head. "This is so not you." She smiled. "I didn't mean that the way it sounded," she clarified.

"I know what you mean." Jay stood. "Come on. I'll show you my little space here in the house. It's my office."

Drew followed her up the stairs, pausing to take a look back at the closed door of Katherine's study, wondering what could possibly be so interesting about old law books. She shrugged. What did she know? Maybe they were fascinating.

"It's small," Jay was saying as she stood by a door, her hand resting on the knob. "Just an extra bedroom I was able to claim." She pushed open the door, waiting.

Drew stuck her head inside and grinned. "Now this is the Jay I know." She went fully into the room, the desk and computer drawing her gaze as she pictured Jay sitting there working. The desktop was littered with swatches, the bookshelf lined with books. She looked around, seeing the recliner tucked into a corner, an old floor lamp beside it. A frayed rug—a Southwestern design—was thrown on the floor, and under the lone window was a small shelf holding four potted plants. Then she saw it and her eyebrows arched. She glanced quickly at Jay, saw the smile, the nod.

"Where did you get it?"

"You like?"

"Can I touch it?"

Jay laughed. "You can look. Keep your grubby hands off."

Drew bent lower, eyeing the helmet, seeing the scribbled signatures on the side. "Wow."

"I was teasing, you know." She lifted up the glass box and took out the mini helmet, holding it carefully by the tiny face-mask. She handed it to Drew. "Here."

"Wow," she said again. "Troy, Emmitt and Michael. The triplets."

"There are fans, and then there are *fans*," Jay said. "Which are you?"

Drew turned the helmet, taking in every detail. "I love the Cowboys," she said quietly. "Everything stops on game day." She looked at Jay. "This is awesome."

"Katherine hates football."

"That's too bad."

"Well, in the past, she would tolerate it and get us tickets to a game now and then. But not in the last several years."

"Some of the builders, they've got season tickets. Maybe I could steal you away one weekend for a game. You think?"

She watched Jay's blue eyes soften, saw the wistful look on her face. Then Jay sighed and brushed at the hair covering her ears, tucking it somewhat nervously behind her ears.

"We'll see."

CHAPTER SEVENTEEN

"You want to come in? Have coffee or something?"

Drew was tired and wanted to go home, but she was curious about the evening, about Katherine, so she agreed. "Decaf?" At the look Jenna gave her, she suspected Jenna assumed—and was hoping—she would decline the offer.

"I think I have decaf, yes."

Once inside, Drew settled at the bar, watching as Jenna poured water into the coffeemaker.

"I enjoyed dinner," Drew said after several moments of silence.

"Did you?"

"Yeah, I did. But I'm wondering what we're doing here."

"What do you mean?"

"You and me. Obviously, there's not anything here," she said, motioning between them. "Yet we've been out four times."

Jenna laughed. "Well, I enjoy spending time with you. What? Do you want to have sex?"

Drew shook her head. "That's not what I meant. But what about you and Katherine?" She was surprised at the quick blush that crossed Jenna's face.

"Oh, God, is it that obvious?" Jenna pulled out another bar stool with her foot and sat down. "And I'm sorry, Drew. I mean, you're very attractive. You're extremely charming." Jenna's smile was nearly apologetic. "But I'm really more attracted to the intellectual type."

Drew's laugh was genuine. She could honestly say no one had ever said those words to her before. "I think I should be offended by that."

"Oh, please don't be. It's nothing against you. It's just, well, Katherine and I had a fling way back when. And when we ran into each other again, the spark was still there. Amazing, but it was."

Drew frowned. "But, wait a minute, Katherine and Jay, they're a *couple*. Right?"

Jenna waved her hand dismissively. "To hear Katherine tell it, they haven't been a real couple in years. In fact, the last time Katherine tried to have sex, Jay would have none of it." She shrugged. "That would turn me off right there."

Drew knew she shouldn't be hearing this, knew she shouldn't ask any questions, *knew* she should just get up and leave. But . . .

"So, you and Katherine are having an affair?" she asked, trying to keep her voice as even as possible.

"Well, I don't know if I'd call it that . . . yet. I mean, we've *talked* about it. How could we not?"

"And tonight, I was just what? A buffer?"

"Oh, Drew, I'm sorry. I should have told you. And we never intended to leave you alone so much, it's just, well, you and Jay seemed to hit if off. We didn't think you'd miss us."

Drew chose her words carefully, surprised at her anger. "I

don't know if *hit it off* is the right phrase, but we have some things in common, have mutual acquaintances in common, yes." She tapped the countertop, staring at the coffeepot. "So I take it Katherine has no intention of telling Jay any of this."

Jenna laughed. "Oh, good Lord, no. Like I said, the spark is still there. That doesn't mean we're ready to run off and get married or anything. We're just taking it slow, seeing what happens."

Drew nodded, not at all sure what to say.

"And, well, you know—if you'd be willing—since you two did hit it off, maybe we could continue to see them together. It would make it easier all around."

"Easier for you and Katherine to sneak off alone?"

"I know it sounds terrible, Drew. But really, you saw them. Did they look happy to you?"

"Well, I'm not certain their relationship is any of my business," she said. And despite how appalled she was at Jenna's suggestion, at their plan, a part of her wanted to do just that. What better way to see Jay? Go as a foursome. It would be perfectly innocent. But she shook her head. In good conscience, she just couldn't do it. Because if Jay found out she'd known, Jay would never forgive her.

"But I guess it is premature to assume there will be other dinner dates. Katherine and I have been meeting for lunch, getting to know one another again. I guess that's enough for now."

But Drew continued to war with herself, thinking how alone Jay would be. What if she hadn't been there tonight? What if they'd just invited Jenna? Would Jay have been left alone to tend to dinner, to tend to cleaning up while the two of them hid in Katherine's office? What would Jay have done?

"Well, I guess I wouldn't be totally opposed to joining you in another foursome," Drew finally conceded. She had a feeling she would live to regret that decision.

CHAPTER EIGHTEEN

"It was the most awkward dinner party I have ever attended," Jay said. "And I gave the damn thing!"

"And you had no idea Drew would be there?"

"How would I? No, Jenna was just bringing a date. Talk about a small world."

Audrey stole the last fry from Jay's plate, then plunged it into her small bowl of mayonnaise. "And after they left, Katherine actually went back to the office? Are you kidding me?"

"And I haven't even spoken to her since. Two days." Jay shoved her plate away and reached for her tea. "I haven't seen Drew either."

"Your life's a crazy mess, you know."

"Why, Audrey, thanks so much for stating the obvious," Jay said dryly. "I can't even get alone with Katherine long enough to ask her if we're over, you know? It's like she can't stand to be around me anymore." Jay lifted her head, staring at the far wall, seeing nothing. "Like she . . . she just can't *stand* me."

"Oh, sweetie, you know that's not true."

Jay shook her head, shocked at the tears that were threatening. "I don't know what to do," she whispered. "She's all I've got."

"Jay—"

"You know what I mean. Eight years, she's taken the place of my family. I live in her house. My car is on her damn insurance, for God's sake," she said. "I let her control my life. I have nothing on my own."

"You have your business."

"Oh, right. My fledgling business with two clients."

"It's taking off," Audrey reminded her.

Jay leaned her head against her hands. "I know. You're right. It's been a good month." She slammed her fist against the table. "But I gave her eight years, Audrey. I have sacrificed for her career, I have given up a lot for her. And to think our relationship has been reduced to *this*, well it just fucking sucks." As Audrey's eyebrows shot to the ceiling, Jay reached across and squeezed her hand. "I know you hate that word. Sorry. But it's the fucking truth," she added with a smile.

Audrey nodded, fighting back her own smile. "I forgive you for your foul language. But I think perhaps you're being too hard on yourself. And you're assuming a lot of things here, Jay. She may have no intention of ending your relationship. She may simply be overworked and not thinking clearly."

"She was thinking clearly enough to make it home for dinner to entertain her old friend, wasn't she?"

"You're jealous of this friend," Audrey stated.

"I am not."

"Of course you are. But are you jealous because of Katherine? Or is it because of Drew?"

"Don't be silly."

"No, you don't be silly. Because frankly, you're going to drive us both crazy with these therapy session lunches."

Jay closed her eyes, fighting back tears. "Katherine is someone I don't know anymore. We're like mere acquaintances on the rare occasions we're together." She opened her eyes. "And Drew, she's like a breath of fresh air. She makes me feel good about myself. So yes, I'm jealous that she's dating Jenna. I'm afraid I'll lose her friendship."

Right? That was all she was afraid of, wasn't it? That Drew would fall in love with Jenna—with anyone—and she would drift out of her life as quickly as she had drifted into it.

Right?

Drew stood in the entry, quietly watching Jay who was sitting cross-legged on the floor, balancing a book in her lap and a handful of swatches in one hand, her glance darting from the book to the wall and back again. Drew's eyes followed her every movement, wondering why she found her actions so adorable. And wondering if she could sneak up on her.

So she tiptoed, much like a child, across the room, unable to wipe the grin off her face as she bent down and quickly covered Jay's eyes with her hands.

"Guess who?"

Jay's scream and subsequent flailing arms sent Drew backward and she landed hard on her ass behind Jay.

"Jesus Christ! I almost peed my pants!"

Drew rubbed the side of her cheek. "Seemed like a good idea at the time."

Jay scooted around until she was facing Drew, both of them still sitting on the carpet. Drew was surprised when Jay reached out and gently touched her cheek, her fingers moving across her skin.

"Did I hurt you?"

Drew shook her head, afraid Jay would move her hand. And she did, her fingers slipping away. But Jay's eyes—God, those eyes—they looked up, holding hers captive.

"You scared me."

"I missed you."

Jay nodded. "Yes."

"Good weekend?"

"No, not really. You?"

Drew shrugged. "Nothing special."

"And Jenna?"

"And Jenna what?"

Jay looked away. "Did she enjoy dinner the other night?"

"Yeah, she did. She and Katherine have been catching up, she said."

"So I hear." Jay got to her knees, then stood. "Where've you been?"

Drew stood too, walking to the wall to inspect the three colors of paint that were splattered on the wall. "We have a couple of new houses. I've been charting the yard, designing the flower beds." She turned. "I like this one best," she said, pointing to the middle paint splash.

"Okay." Jay moved closer, holding up a couple of swatches of burgundy prints. "So which one goes best?"

Drew laughed and backed away. "No way. I'll stick to yards. Color is your thing." Their eyes held as Drew backed out of the room. "See you tomorrow?"

Jay nodded. "Hope so."

CHAPTER NINETEEN

Drew swam lazily across her pool, trying to muster the energy for her normal laps but it was just too damn hot. She ducked her head under the water, enjoying the coolness of the springs, then surfacing again to glide slowly across the water.

She'd been halfway tempted to invite Jay to dinner, even if it was just grabbing a burger at Rhonda's, but she thought better of it. Instead, she'd ask her to lunch tomorrow. It would be safer than dinner. Dinner was too intimate a meal. Lunch, much more informal. Just two friends out for a quick bite. It would be quite innocent.

She flipped onto her back, lazily kicking her feet. If she wasn't careful, this little infatuation she had was going to end up consuming her. And if she had any sense, she'd stay away . . . far away. Her attraction to Jay was reaching levels she was unaccustomed to. Her desire to see Jay, be with her, talk to her, was becoming a force she had a hard time controlling. It was like this unseen energy, powerfully pulling at her, drawing her closer and closer, tightening its grip on her with each encounter.

And making her lose her sense of reality. Because the reality was, Jay was living with Katherine. They were together. They were a couple. For eight years, they'd been a couple. And the reality was that no matter what Drew did, they would still be a couple.

Because even if Jenna and Katherine had an affair—were already having an affair—Jay would never know. She would go on, being as unhappy as she was now, but living a lie with Katherine. And Drew wondered if she pushed the issue, if she kept seeing Jay, would Jay eventually give in to her desires? Would they have their own affair? No. Doubtful. She didn't think Jay was the type. No, they would see each other, flirting with their attraction, much like they did now, driving both of them crazy with it until eventually it had to stop. Jay would pull away, they would drift apart, and their brief friendship would eventually fade.

What a waste.

Drew slipped under the water, her arms and legs moving as they glided under the surface, hands brushing the smooth stones on the bottom as she raced across the pool, trying to outrun her feelings. A waste, yes. Because when she was near Jay, when she looked into her eyes, she knew without a doubt that Jay was the one. The one with all the qualities she sought, the one who held her attention, who made her feel good, who made her heart race . . . the one she longed to touch, to kiss.

She finally surfaced, her lungs ready to burst as she sucked in fresh air. She stood in the water, trying to catch her breath.

She should have told Jenna no, she wouldn't be a part of their so-called foursome. What business was it of hers if Jenna and Katherine had an affair? She wasn't a knight in shining armor. No one expected her to be there should Jay fall, should she need picking up. But how could she, in good conscience, sit idly by, knowing that Jenna and Katherine were sneaking off to be together, leaving an unsuspecting Jay all alone? How could she do that?

"You're gonna get hurt," she murmured. "She's going to break your heart."

CHAPTER TWENTY

Jay punched the remote to the garage as soon as she turned in the driveway, winding through the oak trees toward the back where the garage was. But she slammed on her brakes, frowning. Katherine's BMW convertible was parked inside.

She glanced at the clock on the dash. Six thirty. What in the world was Katherine doing home at this hour? Was something wrong? Was she ill? Questions swirled through her mind as she pulled into the garage and parked beside Katherine's car. Nothing looked out of order, but she hurried through the side door and into the backyard, stopping up short at the sight of Katherine lounging in the pool.

"You're home."

"No, *you're* home," Jay said, going closer. "What's up?"

Katherine lazily splashed water on her legs, putting the float in motion as she drifted toward Jay. "I was tired."

"Yeah, about six months ago."

Katherine laughed. "I made partner. And I met my client goals."

"Congratulations."

Katherine stretched her arms behind her, uttering a satisfied moan as her eyes closed. "So, I'm taking a break. And don't worry about dinner. I've ordered. French okay?"

"Sure."

"Why don't you join me?"

"Okay. Let me change."

"And I'll have another drink," she said, pointing to the empty glass at the pool's edge.

Jay nodded, stopping to collect the glass. She was tired too. She'd had a long day, starting at seven that morning and only breaking for a quick lunch. And she still had work to do. But a dip in the pool sounded refreshing after the heat of the day.

So she shed her clothes, slipping into the sleek, black swimsuit—her favorite. Katherine would say the color wasn't flattering on her, but she didn't care. She refused to wear the bright, flowery one Katherine preferred. She thought it made her look old.

As she made Katherine's drink, she changed her mind on the iced tea she'd already poured. It was hot and she was tired. So she left the gin out, making a Tom Collins for herself too.

"So does this mean you'll be getting back to normal hours?" Jay asked when she joined Katherine in the pool.

"For awhile, yes. Until the end of the year. I think by January, I'll be ready to seriously consider going off on my own. Of course, that'll mean more work as I try to build my own practice. But I've made a lot of contacts." She pulled her long hair behind her, holding the wet ends off of her back. "But I'm ready for a break. And I'm glad you're home. I found us a wonderful place to stay."

Jay frowned, drifting idly in her pool chair. "Stay? Stay

where?"

"In Hawaii. Ten days. And I don't want ten days in a hotel room. How does a bungalow on the beach sound?"

"That sounds . . . sounds lovely. When did you want to do this?"

"Oh, I've already made reservations. Didn't I tell you? The first week in August."

Jay's eyes widened. "August? Kath, you can't expect me to just drop everything without notice. I have deadlines. I'm under contract."

"For what?"

Jay bit her lip. "I have a business, remember?"

"Oh, that. Well, I can't see how ten days can make a difference. Besides, it's still four weeks away. I'm sure you can make arrangements."

And most likely she could. The three houses she'd originally signed on for were all but done. And she knew Kline was about to finish up on another one and she'd most likely get that job as well. But it was just the principle of it all, as if her work was not important. As if she could just put it on the back burner because Katherine decided they needed a vacation.

"I just love the name of the place. *Cedars Under the Rainbow*. There's some sort of legend that goes with it."

"What are you talking about?"

"The bungalows that I've reserved. They're on Maui."

Jay's eyebrows shot up. "Plural? We need more than one?"

Katherine laughed. "Well, Jenna and her date will need one."

Jay was taken aback, shocked by this news. "Jenna? You're planning to invite Jenna?"

"Didn't I tell you?" Katherine asked, waving her hand dismissively. "It's been so great to see her again, but we just don't have time to catch up. I thought this would be the perfect opportunity. Besides, she enjoys a lot of the things that I do. I thought that would let you off the hook."

Jay stared, speechless.

"You can do your snorkeling and water stuff, and Jenna can keep me company while we tour museums and art galleries, and squeeze in some shopping."

"And her *date*?" Jay asked. "I'm to what? Babysit?"

"Well, I assume she'll invite Drew. You two seemed to hit it off the other week at dinner. It won't be like it'll be a complete stranger."

Drew? In Hawaii? Oh, God. "Okay, wait, let me get this straight. You wanted to go to Hawaii because we haven't had much time together lately and you needed a break. Fine. But you're going to invite Jenna and her date so that you'll have someone to do the things you like, and I'll have someone to keep me company while you two are out and about together. Is that the plan?" *Are you kidding me?*

"I think it's perfect. That way I won't have to beg you to get some culture in your life for once and go with me, and you won't expect me to go spear fishing or something equally disgusting."

Spear fishing? Since when have I ever wanted to go spear fishing? Snorkeling, yes. "I guess I'm just a little surprised you'd plan all this without consulting me. I mean, our first vacation in years, you'd think we could both have some input."

"Jay, you're surely not upset about this, are you? I mean, it's a free trip for you. You should be thanking me, not questioning my plans."

Jay stared, at a total loss for words. *Thanking her?*

"We fly out on the second, and we'll pick up a connecting flight in Houston. Ten days in paradise. I hope you're as excited as I am."

Excited? No. How about angry? How about apprehensive? How about scared to death? Ten days with Drew in Hawaii. Drew in a swimsuit. *Oh, God.* She and Drew hanging around together, playing on the beach while Katherine and Jenna did mature, cultural things. Not playing in the ocean like she could imagine she and Drew doing. In *swimsuits*.

"I'm sure it'll be fun," she finally conceded.

"Of course it'll be fun. I can't wait to get away."

Well, so much for her worrying over them spending two weeks together. There would be no lulls in the conversations, no debates over what to do or where to eat, no uncomfortable moments alone. No, they would have none of that. Because they would have *companions* with them. A playmate for both of them. God, how sad was that?

She kicked her feet, setting the pool chair in motion, moving away from Katherine. Katherine didn't seem to notice. She was laying back on her lounge float, eyes closed, seemingly lost in thought. What was she thinking, Jay wondered. Was she mourning the collapse of their relationship? Was she thinking of ways to hold on to it? Did Katherine even *want* to hold on to it? For that matter, did she? Because really, there wasn't anything left to salvage. Was there?

Maybe if they both worked at it, yes, maybe they could salvage it. But Katherine's decision to invite another couple on their vacation—two people who were, in theory, strangers to them—told her everything she needed to know. Katherine wasn't trying to salvage anything. She was trying to make things as stress-free as possible by limiting their alone time together.

Wonder what she'll do when it comes time for bed?

"So what do you say?"

"*Hawaii?* Are you serious?"

"All expenses paid. How can you turn that down?"

Drew stared at Jenna, still shocked by her offer. Ten days in Hawaii. Air fare and lodging paid for. And all she had to do was occupy Jay's time while Jenna and Katherine got to know one another again. "And you're serious?"

"Of course I'm serious. Well, I'm not footing the bill.

Katherine's taking care of all that. My only chore was to talk you into going."

"So Katherine knows you and I aren't really dating?"

"Yes, of course, but she hasn't told Jay that."

Drew rubbed her temples, knowing she really didn't have a choice. If she said no, Jenna would simply find someone else to go. Someone Jay didn't know, some stranger to keep Jay company while the two of them slipped off to be together. In essence, Jay would be alone while her partner of eight years, the woman she lived with, quietly and unceremoniously slithered away to be with Jenna.

How could Drew *not* go? And really, if she was a true friend, how could she *not* tell Jay what was going on? If their circumstances were reversed, she'd want Jay to tell her. She wouldn't want to be played the fool. But that was another problem. As far as Katherine and Jenna were concerned, the one and only time she and Jay had met had been at dinner. Would that be making matters worse if she told Jay what was going on, if Jay then confronted Katherine, if they got into a huge blowup over it all? And if they did end up breaking up, would Jay blame her?

Damn, those tangled webs would get you every time.

So she did what she knew she had to do. She nodded. "Okay, I'm in."

CHAPTER TWENTY-ONE

"Hey."

Jay whipped around, a smile on her face. Drew was in her usual shorts, her tanned legs long and smooth, her work boots dirty and scuffed.

"Hey yourself."

Drew came closer, her eyes twinkling with amusement. "I hear we're going to Hawaii."

"Funny, I heard the same thing."

Drew raised an eyebrow. "And will you be wearing a bikini?"

Jay laughed, her hand unconsciously reaching out to Drew, squeezing her bare arm. "Will you?"

"Would you like me to?"

Jay's breath caught. The question was asked quietly, yet the meaning of those words rang loudly in the room. Jay swallowed, her eyes finding Drew's. "I'm not sure I could stand it," she whispered.

Drew stepped closer, their bodies nearly touching. "If you wear a bikini in my presence, I promise you I won't behave." Her gaze dropped to Jay's lips and Jay nearly moaned. "You know, if I declined to go, Jenna would find someone else. Would you rather do that?"

Jay hesitated, common sense telling her that yes, that would be the safer option. But she didn't even consider it. She shook her head. "No. I'd rather it be you." Jay squeezed her arm again, then took a step back, away from her heat. "I have a feeling we'll be spending a lot of time together."

"Why's that?"

"Katherine and Jenna have exciting trips planned to museums and cute little boutiques where they can shop their hearts out."

Drew made a face. "Museums? Shopping? In Hawaii? Wind surfing, snorkeling, parasailing, *diving*. That's what you do in Hawaii."

"I totally agree. And apparently we'll get to do all those things. Alone," she added.

"That's good. Because I like being alone with you."

Jay fell into her eyes, not even trying to pull away. "We're going to get into trouble, aren't we?"

Drew finally released her, taking a step back, away from her. "No. It'll be fine, Jay. Like I told you, I know what my limits are with you." She smiled. "We'll have fun."

"Will we?"

"Sure."

"And then what, Drew? We come back home and . . . and what?"

"We just come back home, Jay. That's all. We just come back home."

Jay watched her leave, still standing there minutes later, long after she heard Drew's truck drive away. Not only was she struggling with the reality that her relationship with Katherine was unraveling at lightning speed, but she had to face the fact that she had feelings for Drew, feelings that she knew were returned.

Two truths. Katherine moving further and further away from her . . . Drew getting closer and closer. And she didn't have a clue how to deal with either of them.

She slowly reached for her phone, speed-dialing without thought. "It's me." She forced a smile. "You know that Hawaii trip I was telling you about. You'll never believe who's going with us." She paused, nodding. "Thanks, Audrey. I'd love a margarita."

CHAPTER TWENTY-TWO

Drew pressed her face against the window, staring out at the endless expanse of ocean, her gaze traveling to the horizon and back again, seeing nothing but blue-green water. She smiled, remembering her only other trip to Hawaii, a trip given to her for graduation by her grandfather. She'd gone alone, not having any friends who could afford it back in those days. She went alone, yes. She wasn't alone for long.

Her name was Rhea. Tall and dark, she was a surfing lunatic. And Drew had met her that very first afternoon, watching her for over an hour as she surfed the waves on North Shore. Rhea taught her a lot during those ten days. A lot about surfing, a lot about diving, and a whole lot about sex.

She laughed quietly, glancing to her left at Jenna, who was still asleep beside her. Across the aisle of the plane and two rows behind them sat Jay and Katherine. She chanced a look their way. Jay was leaning back, her head turned to the window, her eyes staring outward. Katherine seemed engrossed in a travel guide, her eyes darting across the pages quickly.

She sighed, turning back to her window, again watching the endless passing of water below them. What a crazy month it had been. She and Jay had both been scrambling to complete projects. She was better equipped. Her crews had been with her for years. And in her absence, Johnny would make sure everything ran smoothly. But Jay, she had no one except Connie, a part-time painter and college graduate who wasn't ready to face the world just yet. She didn't blame Jay for worrying. But Randy Kline had been so pleased with her work, he had no qualms with her being gone for ten days, even if the fourth house he'd handed her was not finished.

They'd only seen each other sporadically during the month, meeting a couple of times for lunch. And then the four of them had gotten together at Jenna's place to discuss the trip one night. Now that was a fun night, she recalled.

"Parasailing?" Katherine stared at Drew. "Glide above the ocean as a boat pulls me? You're not serious?" She tossed the brochure aside and picked up another. "Now touring the Royal Palace sounds like fun. Look, Jenna, they actually have an art gallery inside the palace."

"But it's on Oahu. I thought we were on Maui."

"Well, we can hop between islands. That's no problem." She held the brochure up. "How does this sound?"

Drew and Jay exchanged glances. "Boring," they said in unison. Jay held up another brochure. "Look, we can take a tour boat to Molokini," she said. "It's an ancient volcanic cinder cone *teeming* with marine life off the coast of Maui," she read, glancing at Drew. "Best snorkeling on the islands. And diving," she added.

"Oh my, there's the Contemporary Museum on Oahu, as well as the Honolulu Academy of Arts," Jenna said, showing

Katherine the brochure. "That sounds like fun."

Drew smiled, looking back out the window of the plane. *Fun?* Jay had turned to her, her voice low. "I'm *so* glad you're going to be with me."

Yeah. And here they were, finally, on the plane, flying high over the Pacific Ocean, heading to paradise. And, truth be known, she was really looking forward to it. Yes, they would have plenty of time alone. Jenna said she and Katherine planned to use this time to get reacquainted, to see if what they once had was still there. And Drew's job, according to Jenna, was to keep Jay occupied. Not a problem, she'd told Jenna.

How they planned to pull it off though, Drew had no idea. Didn't they think Jay would question them? Wouldn't it look odd if the two of them went off alone? Surely Jay would suspect they were up to no good. And when she did, would she then question Drew's actions? As far as Jay was concerned, she and Jenna were dating. So two couples vacationing on the islands, yet neither of them are spending time with their respective partners. Surely Jay wouldn't just dismiss that.

Drew glanced again over her shoulder, finding Jay watching her. Their eyes held, neither trying to pull away. Slowly, Drew felt her heartbeat increase, felt her shortness of breath, felt the energy between them. What was Jay thinking? But the slight smile, the intense stare . . . Jay was looking forward to this trip as much as Drew was.

And it had nothing to do with Katherine and Jenna.

Oh, yeah, there was going to be trouble.

Jay finally looked away, pulling her gaze from Drew and glancing quickly at Katherine. She still had her nose in her tour book, flipping through the pages like she'd been doing the whole flight. There was no conversation, no visiting. She'd simply been reading. Oh, occasionally Katherine would show her something, flashing a picture at her.

Like now.

"The Big Island has active volcanoes," she said, showing the picture.

"Are you interested?"

Katherine shook her head. "I don't think so. There's Jeep tours and hiking." She smiled. "Sounds more like your thing than mine."

Jay stared at her, wondering when their tastes had grown so far apart. In the beginning, they'd only wanted to spend time alone, with each other. They cooked meals in, rarely going out. They enjoyed each other's company back then. When did that change? When she took the job at Wilkes and Bonner? When Katherine went to work for Miles? Their time together got less and less. And the more Katherine moved up in her world, the further Jay moved down. Katherine was from a prominent family, from old money. She knew all the rules, all the proper etiquette, the right clothes to wear, the best restaurants. And Jay? No, not so much. She was lucky if she knew which fork to use at the fancy restaurants Katherine dragged her to. She rolled her eyes. Really, were four different forks necessary?

And now here they were, only hours from landing in Hawaii, a romantic destination for most. But for them? No. There would be no romance. There hadn't been even a hint of it since Katherine had fallen asleep in the middle of making love a couple of months before. Jay shook her head. No, not making love. Even if they had completed the act, she wouldn't call it making love.

She rolled her head to the side, looking out the window, seeing nothing. Ten days. She would spend much more time with Drew than she would Katherine. That was a given. Katherine already had excursions lined up for her and Jenna. She wondered at Katherine's sudden interest in art, in museums. In all their time together, Katherine never gave more than a passing interest in it. Perhaps it was a passion of Jenna's. Or maybe it was an excuse. Katherine knew, given the choice, Jay would much rather spend her time in the water. So to avoid being around her, she planned things she knew Jay would hate.

Again, that nagging feeling that Katherine just couldn't *stand* to be around her any longer hit full force. Going through the motions took on a whole new meaning. But if that was the case, then what the *hell* were they doing here? Why plan ten days in Hawaii with someone you had no interest being around?

Jay suddenly lifted her head, sliding her glance back to Katherine. *Well, I'll be damned.* They were going to Hawaii because Katherine wanted ten days with Jenna.

CHAPTER TWENTY-THREE

"That's the great thing about time zones," Katherine said as she shut the door on their rental. "We just gained five hours."

Jay glanced at Drew, acknowledging the subtle wink she gave her.

"Oh, this is too quaint, Katherine," Jenna gushed as they walked up the wooden steps to the office. "It's just beautiful."

And it was, Jay admitted. They could hear the waves, smell the ocean, but it was hidden from this angle by row upon row of cedars, most of them dwarfing the palm trees that were scattered about.

"Well, if these are the cedars, where's the rainbow?" Katherine asked with a laugh, her gaze on Jenna.

Jay barely resisted rolling her eyes at Katherine's attempt at a joke. They were saved more trivial chatter when they were greeted by a young lady wearing shorts, sandals and a bright flowery Hawaiian shirt. Completing her outfit was a large red flower tucked behind one ear. Jay wondered if the locals got tired of dressing up for the tourists.

"Aloha . . . welcome," she greeted them. "You must be Katherine Patton from Texas."

"Yes."

"You are right on time. I trust your short flight from Oahu was satisfactory?"

"Wonderful. And the rental car was there as promised."

"Excellent. My name is Eleu. Let me show you to your cottages." She turned to a younger boy standing behind her. She nodded once and he was off, dashing toward their car. "He'll bring your luggage."

They walked through the fragrant garden, alive with vibrant colors of flowers and the lush greenness that Jay could imagine a rain forest having. She took a deep breath, filling her lungs with the sweet smells.

"Wow, look at that."

She looked to where Drew was looking, her own eyes widening. "Wow is right," she murmured, tilting her head up. "And I thought the trees out front were big."

Eleu laughed. "That is the tree of Okalani. Legend has it she planted the tree over four hundred years ago. It draws the rainbows to our island," she said with a smile. "Or so the elders say."

"I was curious about the name of your business," Katherine said. "It makes perfect sense now."

"I will be happy to share the legend of Okalani with you if you are interested."

"Yes. Maybe later," Katherine said. "Right now, I just want out of these clothes and to get into the pool," she said, pointing to the pristine water that shimmered on the other side of the flower garden.

"Of course. But I hope you take advantage of our section of beach here. Your cottages look out over the ocean. It's only a short walk to the water."

"How's the surfing here?" Drew asked.

"Small waves, but a bit rocky in parts. Beginners love it." She looked Drew over. "You don't look like a beginner."

Drew shook her head. "It's been a few years since I've surfed. I think I'd need a refresher course."

"I have brochures of some of the local guides. I can recommend one. But it's farther down the island. The waves are much better."

"Great."

"You surf?" Jay asked as they continued on to their cottages.

"I've been here once before. But it's a story best told over a fruity drink."

Jay chuckled. "I knew there was a reason you were anxious to get to Hawaii. You can drink a mai tai with a cute little umbrella and no one will question your toughness," she teased.

"Can I have sex on the beach too?"

Jay stumbled and Drew grabbed her elbow to steady her, her quiet laugh for Jay's ears only.

"You're very, very mean."

"Here we go, ladies," Eleu said. "These two are yours."

There were only ten or twelve cottages at most, Jay guessed. They sat in a semicircle, all facing the ocean. They were painted different colors, bright fun colors. A back door faced the garden and tiny road, too small for a car. The front door and porch looked out over the beach. Tall palm trees were spaced between each cottage and dozens of flower pots sat haphazardly, all blooming profusely with red and pink flowers.

"The cottages are identical, so take your pick," she said. "Linens and towels are changed daily, usually mid-morning. If you are late sleepers, we can always change our schedule to meet yours."

"Oh, mid-morning is fine," Katherine said. "I do have some excursions planned for Oahu on several days. Can you make the arrangements for transportation?"

"Absolutely. Just let me know when." She looked down the small road, smiling. "Manko is here with your luggage."

The young boy drove a golf cart, their bags piled high around him. Drew rushed over, catching one before it tipped off when he came to a stop.

"Thank you, ma'am," he said shyly.

"No problem. Let me give you a hand." She looked at the others. "Do you guys have a preference?"

"Oh, it doesn't matter," Katherine said. "We'll take this one." She headed to the bright yellow cottage, taking the key from Eleu.

The inside was as bright and airy as the outside. The windows were opened, letting in the fresh ocean breeze, the sheer curtains blowing lazily back and forth. Flowers—most likely cut this morning—were in a vase on the small table. Jay walked to the front door and pulled it open, standing there taking in the view.

"It's beautiful." She turned, finding Eleu watching her. "Everything is beautiful."

"Thank you. I hope you enjoy your stay with us." She turned, pointing to the kitchen. "Everything you need, should you choose to cook here. There's a small grocery store not far from here. They have a wonderful selection of coffee beans." She moved to the lone door. "Through here is the bedroom and bath."

"Thanks, Eleu. I appreciate it," Katherine said. "It's everything you promised."

"Of course. We aim to please," she said with a smile. "I will leave you now. Please let me know what services I can provide."

Manko stuck his head inside, his arms laden with their bags. "The other women said these were yours."

"Yes. Just put them in the bedroom," Katherine said. She turned to Jay. "Didn't I tell you you'd like it? It's costing a fortune, but just having Eleu available to make travel arrangements is worth it."

"Yes. You were right. I think it'll be very relaxing here," she said, ignoring the comment regarding money. She looked out the front door instead. "And the beach is right there." She tossed a glance back at Katherine. "But I don't anticipate you being down at the beach much."

"Oh, I'm sure I'll stroll the beach some and get my feet wet. The water looks crystal clear. I'm more of a pool person, you know that." She laughed. "I prefer to have a cabana boy at my beck and call."

Then why come to an island if you don't like the ocean? Jay shook her head, knowing she had that and many other questions for Katherine, but still she hesitated. She wanted to confront Katherine, wanted to know what was going on. But a part of her *didn't* want to know. A part of her wanted to bury her head in the very lovely sand down on the beach and not spoil their vacation.

So no, she didn't ask. She could go with the flow for a couple of weeks. Because deep in her heart, she knew it was over. She knew it the moment she realized that it was Jenna Katherine really wanted to spend her vacation with. No. That's not true. She knew it was over months ago. It just wasn't so blatantly obvious months ago.

"I'm going to change."

Jay nodded, watching Katherine go into the bedroom, shutting the door behind her. She sighed, leaning her head back with eyes closed. *Gonna be a long ten days.*

"Hey."

She spun around, a smile lighting her face as Drew stood there. No, it wouldn't be so bad. What was she thinking? She and Drew would have ten days to play.

"You're still dressed."

"So are you."

Jay pointed at the closed door to the bedroom. "Katherine went to change. Apparently I wasn't welcome," she said quietly.

"Funny. I got the same treatment."

Jay tilted her head. "Very strange trip."

"I'd have to agree."

Jay walked closer. "They're going to the pool."

"Yeah. Wanna go to the beach?"

Jay grinned. "Absolutely. Meet you out front?"

Drew nodded, her eyes moving over Jay's body. "Bikini?"

"No way."

"Pity."

She disappeared as quickly as she'd come in and Jay's smile faltered once she was alone again. Drew wanted to see her in a bikini. Katherine didn't want to see her at all. Yeah . . . very strange trip.

Jay stopped up short, nearly stumbling in the sand. Drew was waiting, her back to her, staring out toward the ocean, her light brown hair blowing in the breeze. She was wearing next to nothing. And there didn't seem to be even an inch of her that was not tanned a golden brown.

Dear God in heaven.

As if sensing her presence, Drew turned, their eyes meeting for a second before Drew's slid lower. Jay saw the smile form and couldn't prevent one of her own. She hadn't worn a bikini, but her suit left little to the imagination. And thankfully, the time spent in the pool last month had paid off. Her tan was nearly as pronounced as Drew's.

"Beautiful," Drew said, her voice low.

Jay smiled, letting the word sink in. Yes, Drew made her feel that way. Beautiful. Special. Like she *was* somebody, not *nobody*. She flicked her gaze over Drew, her eyes lingering on her small breasts, barely covered by the red top. "That should be illegal."

Drew grinned. "I don't like being in the water with anything on. This was the smallest I could find and still be considered wearing something."

Jay moved closer, surprised at her impulse to touch Drew—her arms, her waist, her shoulder—anywhere to feel flesh. But she controlled her desire, twisting her hands behind her back and looking away. "This is *so* not fair," she said.

"Sweetheart, if you think *your* swimsuit is fair, you're mistaken. And I lied. I *have* undressed you with my eyes."

With that, she turned, jogging easily to the water's edge, leaving Jay staring after her.

We're going to get into so much trouble.

CHAPTER TWENTY-FOUR

"So, we'll meet back here and decide on dinner? That's good with everyone?" Katherine asked early the next morning as the four of them sat by the pool nibbling on fruit and sipping champagne. The table was littered with brochures, and Katherine and Jenna had decided a trip back to Oahu was in order. They just *had* to hit the museums today.

Whatever.

Because Jay decided she wasn't going to worry about it. Yesterday had been a lazy, relaxing day. She and Drew had played in the water, had soaked up the sun, had walked the beach, and finally had joined Katherine and Jenna at the pool. There, they'd spent the rest of the afternoon getting to know Carlos, the very friendly bartender who was spending his first summer there after years of work in his native Cancun. He made a killer margarita. For dinner, Eleu had ordered them an assortment of platters from the nearby Polynesian restaurant. They'd eaten out in the common area near the gardens, meeting some of the other guests staying there. Jay had finally crashed, the five-hour gain finally catching up with her. She had no idea when Katherine had come to bed.

"Sure, whatever," Drew said. She picked up a flyer and held it up for Jay. "Feel like snorkeling?"

"Yes. Anything in the water. I'm game."

Drew raised an eyebrow teasingly and Jay shot a glance at Katherine, but her eyes were on Jenna. She looked back to Drew, wondering if Drew was at all concerned that Jenna, her date, was planning on hanging out with Katherine the whole trip.

"Well, we're off then. Manko is driving us to the airstrip. We'll leave the rental car for you."

"Manko? Is he even old enough to drive?"

"Who cares?" Jenna asked with a laugh, standing. "Come on, Katherine, we don't want to be late."

Katherine shoved her chair back, bending to place a light kiss on Jay's cheek. "You girls have fun. See you this evening."

The smile Jay had forced faded as soon as they were out of sight. She turned to Drew, her brow furrowed.

"You're not really dating Jenna, are you?"

"Not so much, no." Drew stabbed a piece of pineapple. "But she invited me, and well . . . I wanted, well, I thought it'd be good, you know to . . . I mean you and I—hell, I was being selfish."

Jay reached across the table and squeezed her hand. "Thank you. I'm glad you're here." She cleared her throat. "Because I think they're having an affair."

Drew's eyebrows shot up but she kept quiet.

"You think the same thing, don't you?"

Drew nodded. "Yes. I'm sorry."

"No need." Jay stood, moving to the edge of the pool. She took a deep breath, plunging both hands into her hair. She spun around. "Do you mind if we skip snorkeling today?"

"Whatever you want, Jay."

"Yeah? Well, I'd really like to take a very long walk on the beach. I feel like talking." She met her gaze. "Do you mind?"

"Not at all. But is this one of those talks you normally reserve for Audrey?"

Smiling, Jay returned to the table, bending down eye-level with Drew. "It's really you I want to talk to. Not Audrey."

Drew nodded. "I'm all yours then."

The words were spoken casually, lightly, but their double meaning wasn't lost on either of them. As those beautiful green eyes held hers, Jay felt herself being pulled to Drew. And it would be so easy to fall, to let herself go, to trust Drew to keep her safe.

But no. That would only add to the *mess* her life had become.

"I know I led you to believe that my relationship with Katherine was all roses," Jay said later as they walked side by side along the surf.

Their feet were bare, their swimsuits covered by shorts and tank tops. Drew wore a baseball cap, her hair bound and pulled through the back. Her sunglasses were perched on the brim of the cap and she held a water bottle loosely between her fingers. Jay reached for it, pulling it from her grasp and taking a drink.

"I knew it wasn't roses, Jay. I'm not blind."

"Frankly, the last year's been awful," Jay said, handing Drew the water bottle.

"Why have you stayed?"

"Do you leave someone just because they've turned into a workaholic?" Jay shook her head. "She had career goals for herself. I can't begrudge her that. Hell, I have them too."

"But?"

"We've drifted apart." Jay laughed. "God, that's such a cop-out, isn't it? Drifted apart. But the last year, she's stayed at work longer and longer, we see less and less of each other. And this trip," she said, waving her arms toward the water. "She hates the ocean. I should have known something was up."

"Has she said anything to you?"

"No. We don't see each other enough to have those kinds of talks, you know. But her actions speak louder, I suppose."

Drew struggled with her thoughts, trying to figure out what to say, how much to say, trying to figure out how to get out of the proverbial tangled web she seemed to find herself in. She should just tell Jay the truth. No, actually she should have told Jay the truth weeks ago. But then they wouldn't be here, standing on the white sand, watching the clear blue water crash on shore, feeling the ocean breeze against their faces.

"What are you thinking?"

"How selfish I am," Drew said truthfully.

"Selfish?"

Drew stopped walking, facing Jay. "When Jenna asked me to go, I thought it was a little strange, seeing as how we weren't really dating. But I knew it would be a chance to be with you for nearly two weeks." She held her arms out. "Here. Like this. Alone."

When their eyes met, Drew was certain Jay was looking into her soul. She wondered what she saw. Did she believe the half-truth Drew had just shared? Did she think Drew knew more? Could she see the deeply buried desire that Drew had tucked away, far from the surface, thinking it safer to pretend they were just friends, pretend they both weren't struggling with this attraction. *What did she see?*

"When Katherine first told me you were going, I was . . . well, I was terrified." She pulled away from Drew. "Silly, I know. I mean, here I thought Katherine wanted to get away to work on our relationship, and I knew if you were here, that wasn't going to happen. You hold my attention more than she does." She turned back to Drew. "And I guess if I truly wanted to work on our relationship, I'd demand that Katherine and I spend time together."

Drew remained quiet, simply watching Jay struggle with her thoughts.

"I've known for quite some time that I wasn't in love with Katherine." Jay moved, starting to walk again. "But eight years, you know. You don't just throw that away without trying."

"No, I don't suppose you do."

"But it's hard to try when the other party is absent. And I mean absent for days. Oh, she came home to grab a few hours sleep, but that was about it." Jay bent down and picked up a broken shell, fingering it for a moment before closing her fist around it. "And I knew the end was really here when we had dinner with you and Jenna that first night. You see, Katherine never made it home for dinner when it was just me, never took time for lunch if it was me. But for Jenna, she made an exception."

"I'm sorry," Drew said.

"Will you quit saying that? I'm not upset, you know. It's not like this is some big shock to me. I mean, I've lived with it for months now." She stopped, turning to face Drew again. "I've been . . . lonely for months. I don't guess I really realized I was lonely." She looked down, away from Drew. "I didn't like the person I was turning into. I felt broken, defeated . . . lost." She looked up again. "And all those other negative words associated with *failure*."

"So you think it's your fault?"

Jay brushed at the strands of hair that had blown in her face, her eyes steady as she looked at Drew. "No. I don't think it was my fault. Not to begin with. But if I cared, if I truly loved her, why would I let it slip away like it was, like I knew it was? We had half-hearted talks about it, but nothing was ever resolved. I was just told to be patient. And I let it go at that." Jay walked again,

Drew beside her, but she stopped suddenly, her eyes boring into Drew. "How long have you known?"

"Oh, Jay, don't."

Jay reached out to take Drew's hand, squeezing her fingers tightly. Drew shivered. It was the first time they had touched like that.

"If you think that I'm angry with you, Drew, that's not the case. And I know we haven't known each other long, but your eyes," she said, her voice soft, "are like a book to me."

Drew turned her hand, entwining her fingers with Jay's, holding them tightly in her own. She tugged, bringing Jay closer. "And what am I thinking now?"

Jay held her gaze, not pulling away. "You're thinking the exact same thing you thought on the day we met."

"And what is that?"

"You're wondering what it would be like to kiss me."

Drew nodded. "So you *can* read me like a book."

"So tell me, how long have you known?"

Drew relaxed, letting her hand slip away from Jay's. This time, she started them walking down the beach. And this time, she would tell her the truth.

"I asked Jenna about it that night after dinner. She was actually quite embarrassed that I'd picked up on it." Drew looked quickly at Jay. "But she said they weren't having an affair. She said they were *talking*, getting reacquainted. She said there was still an attraction there, and that they were . . . *talking* about it."

Jay nodded but said nothing, still staring off in the distance. Drew stopped her with a light touch on her arm. "I should have said something to you."

"Why? Were they doing anything you and I weren't?"

"Jay, I told you I would never—"

"But we talked about it. We both knew it was there, is still here," she said. "Yet we continue to see each other, to talk, to *flirt* with each other."

"Jay, it's completely different."

Jay took a step closer, her bare legs brushing against Drew's, her face—her mouth—only inches away. "Is it different? How? I could get lost in your eyes, Drew. Just being around you, like this, I feel things I haven't felt in so many years, it's frightening. And I can just imagine how it would be to make love with you. So how is that different?"

Drew couldn't seem to catch her breath, Jay's words stealing it away from her. She came so close, so close to pulling Jay to her, so close to kissing Jay senseless right here on the beach. Jay was daring her to do just that. It took all of her willpower to step away, to put a little space between them. "Point taken," she said, swallowing down the lump in her throat. "But if you do that again, I'll forget all about my promise to you."

Jay, too, moved away. For a second, she rested her face in her hands, then looked up. "I'm sorry, Drew. That was uncalled for."

Drew smiled. "You came very close, Jay." It was her turn to move closer, her turn to tease. "I've made love to you so many times in my dreams, I know exactly what it would be like."

Jay's eyes slammed shut, and Drew heard the low moan that escaped from her mouth, saw the rapidly throbbing pulse in her neck. Again, she just barely resisted putting her lips there. "Very mean," Jay whispered.

"In lieu of a cold shower, how about a dip in the ocean?" Drew didn't wait for a reply. She pulled her tank off and tossed it on the sand, her shorts following. She strode into the surf, diving into the waves, letting the cool water soothe her aching, *throbbing* body, chasing the wanton thoughts from her mind.

Jay stared, watching the tanned, lithe body disappear into the ocean. Only then did she let her breath out, only then did she breathe again.

I've made love to you so many times in my dreams . . .

Jay pulled her shirt off and tossed it next to Drew's. There wasn't any point in hiding, not after the words they'd just exchanged. So she lowered her shorts, pushing thoughts of Katherine aside. As she'd told herself earlier, she wasn't going to worry about it. If what she suspected was true, if Katherine and Jenna were having an affair, were even exploring that possibility, then there was nothing she could do about it.

In truth, she didn't want to do anything about it. It was over. All but the official, verbal declaration . . . nonetheless, it was over.

So she traced Drew's steps into the water, mimicking her actions by diving headfirst into the wave, feeling refreshed and relieved all at the same time. She surfaced, only to have another wave crash into her. She turned her back to the ocean, letting the wave carry her closer to shore, where she could stand. The soft brush against her leg made her gasp, but through the crystal water she saw Drew come up beside her, her body glistening in the sun.

"You okay?"

Jay nodded.

"Do I need to apologize?"

Jay grinned. "Please don't. It's the most sexual activity I've had in months."

"Really? How wonderful."

Jay's reply was lost in the wind as Drew picked her up and held her above the waves, turning circles, making Jay squeal with laughter before Drew tossed her back into the waves. She came up sputtering, reaching for Drew.

"You are dead, Montgomery!"

"You'll have to catch me first!"

CHAPTER TWENTY-FIVE

"I think I like having Eleu order dinner for us, don't you?" Katherine asked as she passed down the platter of cabbage rolls. "I mean, don't get me wrong, I enjoy a fine restaurant as much as the next person, but can you beat this?"

Jay had to agree. The common area in the garden was alive with a fragrance she couldn't even begin to describe. Everything seemed to be blooming at once and the smells were incredible. Top that off with the water garden nearby, the soothing sound of the tiny waterfall, the mynah birds that still sang from the trees, and the sound of the palm trees blowing in the breeze. It was almost an overload to the senses.

"After the busy day we've had, this is wonderful, Katherine."

I bet it was *busy*, Jay thought as she glared at Jenna.

"I actually enjoy this much more than a restaurant any day," Drew said. "For one, you don't have to dress."

Jay glanced at her, hiding her smile. Drew was still in her swimsuit, her feet bare.

"Plus, you know, Carlos is still on duty," Drew added, pushing a tiny paper umbrella aside as she brought the glass to her mouth.

"Yes, Carlos tells me you two have been down here for awhile," Katherine said, looking pointedly at Jay. "How was snorkeling?"

Jay glanced at Drew, hating the fact that she felt guilty. They had done nothing wrong. Well, the tiny bit of flirting, that hardly counted. But Drew saved her from answering.

"We didn't make it. Apparently the boat leaves early. Six. So we just hung out here. The water was great, the sun was great, everything was . . . just great," Drew said, offering a tiny smile to Jay.

"I see. Well, I'm glad you both enjoy the water so much. But I would think you'd get bored just *hanging out*."

Jay frowned, feeling as if Katherine was on the verge of interrogating them. *As if.* "And how was the museum?" she asked, looking between Katherine and Jenna. "Did you enjoy your outing?"

"Oh, yes. Although the Royal Palace wasn't all that. Now the Contemporary Museum, that was quite impressive. They have a good display of Asian art." Jenna looked at Katherine. "But after spending three years in New York, everything else pales."

"It was still interesting."

Jay shot a quick look Drew's way, noting her amused expression as she leaned casually back in her chair. They'd spent the better part of the afternoon sipping on fruity drinks and they were both quite mellow by the time Katherine and Jenna had returned. Jay decided she liked Drew's carefree attitude. And really, after their initial discussion that morning, neither Katherine nor Jenna's name had been mentioned. It was just them, enjoying the day, enjoying each other's company. She didn't really care what Katherine and Jenna did.

"Tomorrow is my day," Katherine was saying. Jay looked up in time to catch the unguarded look Katherine and Jenna exchanged.

"That means shopping, I suppose?"

"Honolulu has some amazing little boutiques. And restaurants. We'll grab lunch." She turned to Jay. "What do you guys have planned?"

Amazing, Jay thought. She could at least *ask* if they wanted to join them. She could at least *offer* to do a joint excursion. So Jay smiled, settling her gaze on Drew. "Actually, tomorrow is Drew's day. Parasailing? Isn't that what you mentioned?"

"Snorkeling in the morning. Parasailing in the afternoon." Drew sat up. "Which reminds me, five o'clock will come early. I think I'll turn in."

"It's not even nine," Jenna said. "Barely dark."

"My body thinks it's two in the morning," Drew said. "Besides, we've been out playing all day. I'm exhausted." She pushed her plate aside and stood. "Thanks for dinner." As she walked past, she lightly brushed Jay's shoulder. "Don't oversleep."

"I won't. See you in the morning." Jay watched her leave, her gaze lingering until she disappeared into the shadows.

"Well, you two seem to be hitting it off," Katherine said. "I suppose you haven't missed me at all."

Jay was at a loss for words. How did Katherine expect her to answer that? The honest answer would be no, she hadn't missed her. "Missed you? Well, Kath, it's not much different than it's been for the last year, is it? I've gotten used to you *not* being around." She softened her words with a smile. "Besides, it saves me having to be subjected to all that *culture*, and saves you a spear fishing event."

But Katherine didn't appear in the mood to be appeased with a smile. "Yes, I know you're limited that way. You wouldn't know *culture* if it slapped you in the face." She, too, flashed a smile. "It seems you and Drew have that in common, luckily."

Oh, my . . . she's in the mood to fight. But Jay was not. She flicked her glance to Jenna instead. "I should thank you for inviting Drew along. She's been a joy to be around."

Jenna nodded. "Yes, she's really nice. I'm glad you enjoy some of the same things. Because you couldn't *pay* me to go parasailing."

Jay laughed. "Well, I haven't committed to it myself. I may end up watching." She reached across the table and took another cabbage roll. "I love these things. What are they stuffed with?"

"Pork and fish, I believe." Jenna took one as well. "I think I'll have another one too. Katherine?"

"No, I'm fine. But it's still early. Maybe we should drive into town and check out the nightlife. Anyone game?"

Jay didn't hesitate. "Not me. I have to be up before dawn. You two go ahead if you want."

"Are you sure?"

"Of course." Jay bit into her cabbage roll, watching them. Did they really think she didn't notice the look and quick smile that passed between them? She wanted to tell them that there was really no need to scheme and plot ways to get alone, no need to try to be conniving. Because she no longer cared.

CHAPTER TWENTY-SIX

"Look at that. Have you ever seen a more beautiful sunrise?"
Drew turned, her glance moving to the red ball of fire just
breaking the horizon, then back to Jay. The early morning shadows still danced across her face, but the pink rays of light
reflected off her blond hair, causing an amber glow. Within seconds, Jay was totally engulfed by the sun as it rose—seemingly
right out of the water—a pillar of red and orange light streaking
across the ocean, finding Jay in its sights. Jay turned, pulling her
gaze from the sunrise, looking at Drew expectantly. There was
no guarded look on her face, nothing she was trying to hide. And
in that moment, that glance, Drew knew she had fallen in love.

She saw the recognition in Jay's eyes, saw the surprised
expression cross Jay's face. Yes, Jay knew it too.

"No, I've never seen anything more beautiful," Drew whispered. She wanted to close the distance between them. She

wanted to touch her . . . kiss her. But then their surroundings came alive, the boat rocked gently on the water, the crew and other passengers moved about, all admiring the sunrise with them. The spell was broken.

So she was surprised when Jay came closer, surprised at the warm hand that moved across her skin, resting on her arm. Surprised at the look in Jay's eyes.

"I will forever remember that sunrise, forever remember the way you just looked at me."

"I want to make love to you," Drew said, saying the words that were aching to come out.

Jay closed her eyes, her fingers tightening on Drew's arm. When she opened them, Drew saw her desire mirrored there. Then Jay smiled, letting her hand slip away. "Maybe we should start with something smaller. Like a kiss." Jay took a deep breath and moved away. "Because I really want to kiss you."

"This was a great idea," Jay said as they rested in the shallow waters of the reef, the island crater of Molokini protecting it from the ocean waves. She blew air into her snorkel, getting out the last of the water. "I can't believe how clear the water is."

"Yeah. I wish I'd thought to get a camera. The fish are incredible."

"I really want to see an eagle ray. Actually, I'd want to see a manta ray, but I heard one of the crew telling someone that their wingspan can get up to thirty feet." Jay laughed. "You could very well see me walk on water if I encounter one of those."

"From what I remember, manta rays are very docile. And unless we're diving, I doubt we'll see an eagle ray." Drew dipped her mask in the water, then shook it out. "Do you dive?"

"I would need a refresher course. I took lessons several years ago. One of the guys I worked with at Wilkes and Bonner loved scuba diving. He talked me into lessons, but we only went out to the lakes around Austin." Jay slipped her mask on her head. "Did you dive when you were here before?"

"Yeah." Drew grinned. "I had a personal teacher. She taught me to surf, snorkel and dive. Among other things."

Jay watched her disappear under the water, her tiny red bikini easy to follow in the crystal clear waters. She adjusted her mask and snorkel and followed, getting lost in the underwater paradise.

"Are you sure you're okay with this?" Drew asked as she strapped on her scuba gear.

"Of course. I'll hang out on the boat. I'll be fine."

And actually, she was too stuffed to attempt more water activities after they'd been served a barbequed lunch on board. They had another hour before the boat would take them to Turtle Town, an area with a colony of sea turtles. For that, she might get back into the water. The crew had told them the turtles were used to humans and swimming among them should not be missed.

Drew and three others crawled into the small inflatable raft that had been towed behind the boat. One of the crew sped them away, bouncing over the waves as they headed to the back side of the crater to do some diving. Jay watched them for a moment, then headed down. She thought she'd at least take advantage of the glass bottom. There were only four others mingling, walking along the railing and pointing out the colorful fish.

She took a seat, leaning back and stretching her legs out. She closed her eyes, wondering how long she was going to go on pretending this vacation was perfectly normal. Not that she'd rather be spending time with Katherine instead of Drew. That wasn't the case. But the whole situation was surreal. She and Katherine not speaking, Jenna and Drew barely seeing each other, their strained conversation at dinner. She wondered if perhaps

Katherine was doing it intentionally, hoping Jay would be the one to bring it up, the one to question their relationship, the one to end things. Is that what she wanted? For Jay to be the bad guy?

No. That wasn't Katherine's style. She was always the aggressor. If she wanted to end things, she'd just do it, regardless of how it affected Jay. Which brought up the question, why was she sneaking off with Jenna? After their conversation at dinner last night, after Katherine and Jenna went off to enjoy the nightlife—alone—and after Katherine had slipped into their bed in the wee hours of the morning, doing her best to avoid even touching Jay, why would she go to the trouble of hiding this?

Does she think I'm totally clueless?

Or most likely Katherine . . . like Jay . . . just didn't want to have this great big dramatic scene here in paradise, didn't want to spoil everyone's vacation.

Didn't want all *this* for a backdrop when ending their relationship.

CHAPTER TWENTY-SEVEN

They sat on the sand, legs outstretched, watching the approaching sunset in silence. It had been a full day, a good day. There was no mention of Katherine or Jenna, no mention of where they were or what they were doing, and no mention of the *affair*.

Which was fine with Drew.

Because the day had been too perfect. From the sunrise, the snorkeling and playing, the lunch they'd shared in a quiet corner of the boat, the swim with sea turtles—which Jay absolutely loved—and now, a few quiet moments alone as they sat side by side, waiting for the day to end.

"Good day?" she finally asked, watching as Jay continued to stare out over the water.

Jay turned, gently bumping Drew's shoulder with her own. "Yeah, great day. You?"

"I loved it. I'm tired, but I loved it."

"So when are you going to tell me about this personal teacher you had?"

Drew grinned. "She was something else. Rhea. My trip here was a gift from my grandfather when I finished college. I'd always loved the water, but my exposure to all this," she said, waving her hand to the ocean, "was a handful of trips to Galveston Island. And it couldn't even begin to compare. When I stood on North Shore and watched the giant waves come in, I was terrified. But then I saw her. Long raven hair, her body bronzed, head to toe." She laughed. "I found out later that it was indeed head to toe."

Jay laughed too. "What were you? Twenty-one? Twenty-two?"

"Yeah. And she wasn't much older. And she could do anything. We went snorkeling and diving. We went kayaking out in the surf. Windboarding. And then one day she brought an extra surfboard. And we spent the entire day in the water, her teaching me the basics of surfing."

"And when did the basics of the bedroom come into play?"

"Dare I say the first night?"

"Oh, you're so bad," Jay teased.

"Yeah, I was. We were together for ten days, day and night. I was exhausted," she said with a laugh. "I think I slept two days straight when I got back home."

"And home was your grandfather's place?"

"Yeah. My grandmother had passed away the year before, so it was just the two of us."

"You talk about your grandfather, but you don't really mention your parents."

"Well, like I told you, I don't see them much. Christmas, that's about it." Drew looked out over the water, memories crowding in as she watched the sun touch the horizon. "My dad was ill, always had something wrong," she said. "So my grandfather, well, he was everything my father wasn't." She glanced quickly at Jay. "Plus, I think they gave up parenting when I came along. I mean, I wasn't the son they'd hoped for." She scooped up a handful of sand and let it flow from her fingers. "Don't get me wrong, I didn't have a crappy childhood or anything, but I was never challenged. I went to school, did my homework and that was that. I wasn't ever pushed to do more, to do better. I was just left alone. If I passed, I passed. If I didn't, no big deal. But during the summer, I'd go to Austin to stay with my grandparents. All summer long. From the day school let out until it started up again. And there were always projects and activities, and he let me help him in his nursery, and then there was the pool." She pointed toward the sun, and Jay nodded, her eyes moving from the orange ball then back to Drew. "Anyway, you should see his pool. Well, my pool now. It's spring-fed. He found it quite by accident. They were digging, trying to level out an area where he was going to put a garage, of all things." She smoothed out the sand with her hand, then drew an elongated S. "It's like this," she said. "It's got a limestone bottom, and it's all stone around the edges. No concrete."

"Sounds lovely."

"You'll love it. It's so lush. There's stuff growing all around it. It's like swimming in the forest."

"And knowing you as I do, I'm guessing you swim nude."

"Of course. Is there any other way?"

They were both quiet, watching in silence as the sun slipped from their sights, leaving behind a swirl of orange and red that rode the ocean waves back to shore, leaving the colors lapping at their feet as the waves retreated back to the sea.

"Perfect way to end the day," Jay murmured. She sat up, curling her arms around her knees and resting her cheek there. "But I suppose we should get back."

"Yeah. Wonder if they even miss us?"

Jay shook her head. "I'm guessing not." She sighed, then lifted her head. "You knew they went out last night, right?"

"I assumed, since it was very late when Jenna came in."

"I'm not sure how much longer I can take this." Jay looked away. "It's just so crazy to keep on pretending nothing out of the ordinary is going on."

"You're ready to confront her?" Drew asked.

"I'm ready for her to be honest with me. I'm ready to end this charade."

Drew nodded. There wasn't much of a charade on her part. She and Jenna spoke even less than Jay and Katherine. And they weren't sharing a bed. Each night, Drew pulled open the sofa and made up the queen-sized bed, further evidence that she was only here for the sake of appearances.

"Do you want me to say something to Jenna?"

Jay shook her head. "No. You and Jenna shouldn't be involved."

"I think it's too late for that."

Jay sighed. "You're right. I guess I should just enjoy the time I have with you and not worry about them. I just hate it that she thinks she's being so discreet with this affair. She must think I'm a complete idiot."

The colors had nearly faded from the sky and dusk was upon them. They should get back, Drew knew. But really, did she care? She was more interested in sitting here with Jay, more interested in how Jay felt, what she was thinking.

"Are you ready to let her go? Do you want to fight for your relationship?"

Jay smiled. "Are you asking for yourself or as a concerned friend?"

"Can I say both?"

Jay nodded. "If this was six months ago, I'd say I would fight." She turned her gaze to the darkening sky. "But it's not six months ago. And I can accept how unhappy I've been." She turned her head, looking at Drew. "And you weren't in my life six months ago."

"What if I wasn't in your life now?"

"I'm not sure. I mean, our relationship for the last year hasn't exactly been a good one. But I think it took meeting you for me to realize how completely different Katherine and I are. We were going through the motions, that was all. We never talked anymore. I can't imagine being on this trip, just the two of us. We wouldn't last a week."

"And when we get back?" Drew asked. "Then what?"

"What do *you* want, Drew?"

Yes, what did she want? Did she want to go through the ritual of dating? They'd known each other a handful of months. They'd been to lunch together, to dinner. They'd seen each other at their respective jobs. Jay had seen her with mud and dirt up to her elbows, and she'd seen Jay with dirty shorts covered in paint stains, her hair disheveled from her habit of running her hands through it, paint and all.

No, she didn't think the ritual of dating was necessary. But she couldn't very well ask her to move in with her, could she? So she said what she thought was expected.

"I want to be able to see you, to go out. I want to have the right to look at you and not have to worry if someone sees me."

Jay laughed. "And here I thought you'd say you wanted to take me up to one of the cottages and have your way with me."

But Drew didn't laugh. She turned, moving around to face Jay, watching her face in the shadows. "I want to make love to you, yes. I want to touch you and kiss you," she said quietly. "But I didn't think you wanted to hear that." She took her hand. "Jay, since the day I met you, I've had this . . . this thing. God, I can't even describe it without sounding like a complete idiot."

"Try."

"It's like, I looked into your eyes and I was possessed by you. Like Cupid's arrow got me. Like a siren's song pulling me to you. All of those things, Jay. And it takes all of my willpower not to touch you. Because you're not free."

Jay reached between them, her palm soft against Drew's face.

Drew closed her eyes, loving Jay's touch.

"I don't want to be like them, Drew. I don't want to sneak off with you. I don't want to have an *affair* with you. That's not what you want, is it?"

Drew shook her head.

"Because if you did," Jay continued, "I'm not sure I could resist. But I don't want that to be our defining moment, Drew. How could you ever trust me again?"

"What do you mean?"

"If they're having an affair, then it's okay if you and I do too? That's our justification? Because if, in the future, you and I should ever have something, be together, would you always remember that? I know it's a cliché and all, but would you always wonder if I was capable of doing that to you? I mean, I did it once, right? Katherine and I haven't discussed *anything* about our relationship. Yet here I am, with you, talking about making love."

"Jay, I don't want you doing anything you're not comfortable with. This whole situation is just crazy, anyway. Us being here in Hawaii, them going off on their own as if it's perfectly normal, and these feelings that we have for each other, yet . . ." Drew took Jay's hand again and brought it to her lips, kissing it softly. "I want what you and Katherine had. I want to be the one you come home to. I want to be the one you make love to. But right now, that's not possible. Because Katherine met you first. And whatever you have to resolve with her, whatever the outcome, I have to accept it. I told you months ago that I knew what my limitations were. And I do. You're in a very long relationship with her. You're not available to be courted," she said with a smile. She kissed her hand again, her lips lingering. "And I didn't have the right to fall in love with you."

"Oh, Drew," Jay whispered. She touched Drew's face again, her thumb rubbing lightly across her lips. "All this and we haven't even kissed."

"I don't think I could stop with a kiss, Jay."

CHAPTER TWENTY-EIGHT

"I can't believe we're having pizza," Katherine said as she reached for a piece. "I mean, really, we can have pizza in Austin. Is this the best Eleu could come up with? Have we run out of authentic dishes already?"

Jay and Drew exchanged glances, Jay noting the amused twinkle as Drew took a huge bite. "Well, you guys weren't back yet," Jay said. "And we were starving." She grabbed her third piece. "If you want something else, just let Eleu know. I'm sure she won't mind."

"No, it's getting late. I suppose this will be fine. I'm ready for an early night myself."

"Really? I thought you might want to hit the town again tonight." Jay took a sip of the margarita Carlos had made for her earlier. "How was it, anyway?"

"Oh, we had a great time," Jenna said, her smile beaming.

"We found a nightclub that was made up to look like a Seventies disco. Totally amazing."

"Disco?"

"Oh, yes. It was so much fun," Katherine said. "It was all original disco music. We had a blast."

"Disco?" Jay asked again. "You like *disco*?"

"Well, its heyday was before my time, without question, but I still remember the music."

"And I'm really sorry I missed it," Jay said, her voice dripping with sarcasm. "Did you get your shopping out of the way today?"

"Oh, God, we hit every boutique on the island, I think," Jenna answered. "Surely she's had enough." She softened her words with a laugh, but Jay wondered if perhaps Jenna had been overwhelmed. She'd been on a shopping spree with Katherine years before. She swore she'd never go again.

"Can you ever do too much shopping?" Katherine smiled politely at Drew. "What did you two do today?"

"Snorkeling. We took a tour boat out to Molokini. On the way back to shore, it stopped at Turtle Town and we were able to swim with sea turtles. Totally awesome."

"Sea turtles? Yes, how *totally awesome*," Katherine repeated, her face showing her disgust in case her words did not. "Sorry I missed that."

Jay ignored Katherine, sliding her gaze to Drew instead. "Biking tomorrow?"

"If you're up for it." Drew looked from Katherine to Jenna. "A tour bus hauls you up to the top of a volcano and you bike back down. It's like a forty degree temperature difference."

"What island?" Jenna asked.

"Here on Maui. Haleakala. It's a national park. There's a rain forest, four hundred foot waterfalls, freshwater swimming. They haul you to the top to catch the sunrise, then you bike back down about thirty-eight miles."

"Oh, my God. You're not serious?" Katherine asked. "Thirty-eight *miles?*"

"It's all downhill," Jay said.

"That's insane."

Drew laughed. "What's insane is having to be at the tour company by four a.m."

"Please don't wake me when you leave," Katherine told Jay. "We don't have anything nearly as strenuous planned."

"And we thought you guys might want to join us," Jay said. "You know, get out and do something."

"Not my cup of tea, but thanks," Katherine said. "Actually, we're going back to Oahu again. This island hopping is quite fun, isn't it, Jenna?"

"Oh, sure. And we're going to do the touristy thing tomorrow and do Pearl Harbor."

If there was one touristy thing Jay wanted to do while here, it was to visit Pearl Harbor. And Katherine knew it.

"You are?" Drew looked at Jay. "Wow. That's something I wanted to see for sure. Didn't you?"

Jay nodded. "I did."

"Well, I doubt you'd want to go with us," Katherine said quickly. "We're going to the Honolulu Academy of Arts beforehand. And with luck, get tickets to the theater afterward."

Jay wondered if she was telling the truth or had just made that up on the spot, knowing she and Drew would decline.

"Maybe we can go another day then." Drew raised her eyebrows. "Jay, that good with you?"

"Sure."

"We could make a day of it. I'll show you North Shore and Waikiki."

Jay smiled, ignoring the others. "And did you give thought to looking up Rhea?"

Drew laughed. "I don't think I could keep up with her now."

"Who's Rhea?" Jenna asked.

"Oh, she was a girl I met when I came over here after college.

She taught me some . . . water sports."

Jay laughed. "That's the best you can come up with? Water sports?"

"Wow. She must have been something," Katherine said dryly, glancing between Drew and Jay. "I had no idea you'd been here before."

Drew shrugged. "Years ago. It was a graduation gift."

"How nice. I went to Europe for my graduation." Katherine smiled at Jenna. "Then back to Italy after law school. What did you do?"

"Nothing that exciting. I met my mother in New York, and then we took a quick trip to London. It's a little hard to let loose with your mother in tow."

Jay wanted to be angry at the callousness of these two, but Drew didn't seem the least bit fazed by it. She simply took another piece of pizza, ignoring them. But Jay had had enough. She stood, moving away from the table. "Gonna call it a night, guys. I want a hot shower." She looked at Drew and smiled. "Three a.m.?"

"Three. Do you think we can find a coffee place that early?"

"I'll make some in the cottage. We can take it with us." Jay turned to Jenna. "Goodnight."

"I'll try not to wake you," Katherine called as she walked away.

CHAPTER TWENTY-NINE

"My God, whose idea was this?" Jay asked as she handed Drew her coffee.

"I think it was yours," Drew reminded her, closing the door quietly behind her. "Did she wake?"

"No. Or if she did, she didn't let me know. Yours?"

"No. But you know, I'm sleeping on the couch, so it wasn't that hard."

Jay stopped in her tracks. "The couch? You're not even sharing a bed?"

"No. Why would you think that?"

"Because you're supposed to be *dating*," Jay said. "Does she know that I know that you're not dating?"

"No."

"Crazy as hell trip," Jay murmured as she headed to the rental. "You drive. It's far too early for me to get behind the wheel."

Jay sat silently in the car, sipping her coffee, watching the dark road ahead as Drew drove them across the island. There were few other cars about this time of the morning, and those that were traveling, she wondered what their destination was. Fishermen heading to the boats? Other tourists like them, heading out for an early morning excursion?

"You okay?"

Jay yawned and nodded. "Just not used to getting up at three in the morning. Even the cold shower I took didn't help much." She turned in her seat, watching Drew's profile. "Do you know where you're going?"

"Eleu gave me directions. It's only one block off of the main road here. I think we'll be fine."

"Do you bike?"

"Not so much anymore. I've got a road bike and a mountain bike, and I'll take one out for a spin occasionally. What about you?"

"Not since . . . well, since I met Katherine. When I was still in Lubbock living in the dorms, I rode all over campus. And even when I first moved to Austin, I'd go out to the greenbelt. But Katherine, well, as you can tell, she's not exactly the sporty type. That kinda fell by the wayside, and by the time we moved in together, I'd gotten rid of my bike." Truth was, she had given up a lot of things for Katherine. Things that, at the time, didn't seem all that important. But Katherine was never very flexible when it came to how they spent their time. She had a much more domineering personality than Jay and it was simply easier to agree than to argue about it. Which is why, over the years, they had stopped doing as much together. Jay found little enjoyment in shopping for hours on end and was more than happy to send Katherine out alone on one of her sprees. And season tickets to the theater? No, thank you. An action film with surround sound at the new movie theater, a bucket of popcorn and a large Coke was much more to Jay's liking. And as she'd told Audrey many times, she'd rather have a root canal than sit through another boring lecture at the university. The lone activity they both enjoyed doing—walking the hike and bike trail at Town Lake—came to an end years ago when work took up more and more of their time.

Drifted apart? That was an understatement. Although, if she were honest about it, *she* was the one who had drifted. Not Katherine.

"Here we are," Drew said, interrupting her thoughts.

Haleakala Bike Tours was lit up, the parking lot bustling with activity. "Do you think we're late?"

"No. We still have a half hour."

Drew pulled in next to a red Jeep and cut the engine. Jay turned, smiling at her. "I can't remember the last time I've been this happy at three thirty in the morning."

Drew laughed. "I'd have to agree with you. Now if only the sunrise cooperates."

They grabbed their backpacks and headed inside, where they were met by an enthusiastic young man with long beaded hair and a tidy goatee.

"Welcome, welcome to the morning," he said, urging them inside. "You have reservations?"

"Yes. Drew Montgomery, Jay Burns."

"Of course, of course. I am Gregory. Come quickly. We will get you fitted. The sun will not wait on us." He hurried them to a wall of bikes, all different colors and sizes. He looked Drew up and down. "Five-nine, yes?"

Drew grinned. "Yeah."

"Good, good." He pulled out a sleek bike. "Perfect for you." He turned to Jay, studying her much like he'd done Drew. "Five-seven?"

Jay smiled. "Thanks for the extra half-inch."

But he frowned and shook his head. "I never miss. Must be

the shoes." He walked down the row, bending to inspect two bikes before selecting one for Jay. "Here. Perfect for you." He pointed across the room. "Go. You'll need a jacket for the summit. And gloves, if you wish. It's cold at the top. Okana will help you. You'll get water bottles and a map once we're there."

"I think he's had too much caffeine," Jay teased as they headed to the jackets.

It was still completely dark when their van pulled to a stop near the summit. There were two vans with ten riders on each. Drew and Jay were the first ones off and they stood near the back, waiting for Okana to unload their bikes.

"Two water bottles, everyone," Gregory announced. "Once it is daylight, you can check your maps. There is a spring about halfway down. It is safe to drink. The locals come to get water there. You may fill your water bottles without worry. Don't drink the water anywhere else though, no matter how clear it looks. Our vans will meet you at the bottom. You have until noon to explore the mountain. And take your time. You'll be down the mountain in a flash." He looked them over in the low lights of the van. "Any questions?"

"How many miles is it?" someone asked.

"Thirty-five from here. All downhill. You will rarely even need to pedal. The summit is about three miles up ahead. Feel free to explore it. All uphill." He waited, but no one else asked any questions. "Great. After the sunrise, daylight comes quickly. Have fun, my friends. And be careful."

As soon as the red taillights of the vans disappeared, the group of bikers dispersed. Some already beginning the trek up to the summit, but most others staying to catch the sunrise. Drew led Jay away from the others, finding a flat rock to sit on. They leaned their bikes against a tree, then sat side by side, their gazes looking out over the ocean to the east, far below them.

"How high are we?" Jay asked quietly.

"I don't know. I think I read where the summit is around ten thousand feet, so I guess we're about eight or so."

Jay leaned closer. "Because it's cold."

"Yeah. Hard to imagine we'll be shedding these clothes before long."

Drew opened her coat and slipped an arm around Jay, pulling her nearer to her warmth. Jay didn't hesitate as she snuggled closer. She wasn't *that* cold. But damn, it felt good to be this close to her.

They sat quietly, the sky lightening now, hinting at the colors that would come. Jay tried to concentrate on the sunrise, tried to keep her mind in a sane place, but her body wanted to get closer, and she shivered, not from the cold, but from the heat of Drew's body.

"Still cold?"

"No. This is nice." Jay reached between them, taking Drew's hand. It was as cold as her own, but she was thankful they hadn't bothered with gloves. She ran her fingers across Drew's skin. Her hands were smooth, but her fingers hinted at calluses, evidence of her occupation. "I like your hands," Jay said.

"They're not very soft. Working hands."

"Yes. That's what I like."

They were quiet again, both staring at the sky, watching as the very tip of the sun broke the horizon. Drew squeezed her hand, both waiting for the explosion of color they knew would greet them. They didn't have to wait long. The dull red orb rose out of the water, the dullness changing to a brilliant shine as the color turned to burgundy before taking on a hint of orange. Colored light blasted out in every direction, shooting across the ocean in waves, turning the placid blue-green into a fiery cauldron as the colors raced to the shore.

"So beautiful," Jay murmured. "My God, so damn beautiful."

"Mmm."

Jay leaned closer, resting her head on Drew's shoulder as the sky came alive with colors. "I think I want to be on a date," she said.

Drew squeezed her hand. "Is that right?"

"Yeah. I feel . . . *normal* with you. Does that make sense? I'm more myself. I recognize *me* when I'm with you. I'm not just some foreign entity drifting about, trying to be something else. I'm just me."

Drew turned, brushing her lips across Jay's hair. "You can always be yourself with me. There's not anything you need to hide."

Jay smiled and moved away. "Yeah, right now I have to hide the fact that I want to kiss you. Kiss you a lot." She stood, her gaze traveling to the sun, the deep red colors being replaced with orange. Soon it would rise higher, the colors fading completely. And Gregory was right. Daylight came fast up here. The shadows had disappeared and so had some of the riders. There were only a handful of others still about, some discussing whether they wanted to climb to the summit, others looking at the map, deciding where to explore first.

She felt Drew walk up beside her and she turned, liking the contented look on Drew's face. She held up the map.

"The first waterfall trail is not too far from here," she said, showing Jay the map. "Interested?"

"Yes. Anything."

"Anything?"

Jay cocked her head. "Yeah, anything."

"Well, I'd really like to swim in one of the natural pools. Three of the waterfalls have them. What do you think?"

Jay laughed. "I swear. I give you an opening and you want to go swimming."

Drew wiggled her eyebrows. "Didn't I mention it would be nude swimming?"

"Not on your life." Jay tugged her arm. "Come on. Let's work some of this energy off."

Of course coasting downhill didn't really require much energy except riding the brake, which Jay was doing now as they sped around a curve, the cool wind blowing against them. The forest was a blur as Jay kept her eyes glued to the road . . . and Drew's backside.

"The trail's up ahead," Drew called over her shoulder.

Jay slowed, her hands squeezing hard on the brakes. She followed Drew, easing to a stop along the side of the road. A well-marked trail led into the forest. A muddy trail. Jay looked down at her blue and white Nikes.

"Yeah, I'm thinking the same thing," Drew said. "Maybe we should try the next waterfall."

And they did. Just a short while later coming to another trail, this time on the other side of the road. And this time a dry trail.

"Why was the other so wet?" Jay asked as she leaned her bike against a tree.

"They're on opposite sides. It's like a mountain range. The storms come from one direction, dropping moisture, but the peaks shield the other side. I guess here, the eastern side catches the rain and west does not."

"Then the waterfalls must be spring fed," Jay guessed.

"Which is why I'm dying to go swimming in them." Drew pulled off her jacket and stuffed it in her backpack, but left the wind pants on.

Jay unzipped her jacket, but kept it on, the morning wind still chilling her. "Will our bikes be okay here?"

Drew shrugged. "They didn't give us any chains or locks, so I imagine it's okay. Besides, I don't think anyone else is up here this early other than our tour group."

"Okay. Then lead the way."

"It's not too far," Drew said as they followed the trail into the forest.

"I'm fine. I enjoy hiking. But judging by this manicured trail,

I don't believe we can really call it hiking."

They both stopped a short time later when they heard the roar. Drew grabbed Jay's arm, her head tilted as she listened.

"It's almost as if the ground is vibrating."

"It's deafening."

They walked on, the trail literally dumping into a fenced overlook, the waterfall's roar blocking out all other sound. They were so close, they could feel the spray as it tumbled past them some four hundred feet down, forming one of the swimming pools Drew wanted to visit. There were no words to describe it and Jay didn't even try. She simply stared at the massive wall of water that plummeted by at lightning speed. She turned to Drew, their eyes meeting for a second before looking back to the waterfall.

And how long they stood there, Jay didn't know. She felt Drew's fingers entwine with hers, felt the gentle tug. She blinked, realizing she was almost in a trance. There were no thoughts running through her mind, no words, nothing. She merely stared, absorbing the sight.

She finally nodded, following Drew back the way they'd come. When the roar subsided, Drew turned, excitement still showing on her face.

"Can you *believe* that? We were *right* there. How cool was that?" she asked excitedly.

Jay laughed. "God, that was *awesome*. We were so close to it, we could almost touch it."

"Can you imagine swimming at the bottom of that thing?"

"No."

Drew grinned. "Yeah, neither can I." She motioned with her head. "Come on. Let's see what else we can find."

And they did, finding four more falls on their way down, each matching the beauty of the one before. But none could match the intensity of the first one. By the time they'd hit their third, they both had shed their wind pants and were riding in shorts

165

and T-shirts, cruising down the mountain at breakneck speed, turning into each curve like they'd done it hundreds of times before. At the fourth waterfall, Drew found her swimming hole.

The view of the falls was from down below, and they lifted their heads, looking high above them where it fell off the mountain.

"I'm ready for that swim now, if you are," Jay said, pulling the T-shirt away from her neck to let air in.

"Yeah. Let's hike this one down. It doesn't look far."

And it wasn't. They took their bikes with them a short ways, tucking them into the forest beside the trail before heading down. They could hear the water splashing on the rocks long before they got there, and it was as the brochure promised—a freshwater swimming pool at the base of a four-hundred foot waterfall.

"Oh, my God," Jay said as she turned in a circle, her head looking up to where the falls began. "Tell me again why the hell we don't have a camera?"

Drew grinned. "That's a rhetorical question, right?"

"Who comes to Hawaii without a camera?"

"Apparently us," Drew said as she pulled off her T-shirt, her tiny red bikini top barely covering her breasts.

Jay stared. "Red is definitely your color."

"Yeah? And what are you wearing today?" She came closer, lifting Jay's shirt up, exposing her tanned belly.

Jay stood still, letting Drew pull her T-shirt over her head. She stood in front of her, her black top covering nearly as little as Drew's. She watched Drew's face, saw her eyes darken. Drew's eyes traveled over her, leaving her breasts, meeting her own gaze.

"You wore a bikini," she said quietly. "That is so not fair."

Jay took the shirt from Drew's fingers with a smile. "Paybacks are hell."

"I only hope the water is cold."

And it was, both of them gasping when they jumped in. Jay moved into the sun, but the pool was deep. She finally found a rock to stand on as she treaded water, lifting her face skyward.

"Cold, but so refreshing." She shook her hair out. "This is beautiful."

Drew swam over, moving into the shallow water, watching her. Jay saw her gaze slip to her breasts, saw her lips part slightly. It was then she realized what held Drew's attention. Her nipples were rock hard. From the cold or Drew's nearness, it didn't matter. She could feel them straining against her black bikini top, could feel Drew's eyes on them.

"Drew Montgomery, behave yourself," she teased, splashing water at Drew.

Drew laughed. "Sorry. I'm a pig, I know." She ducked under the water again, swimming away, giving Jay room.

Jay took a deep breath, her hands cupping herself, squeezing her breasts, feeling her nipples dig into her palms. She and Drew were getting closer. Every day, every glance, every innocent touch . . . they were getting closer. How long could they deny what was so painfully obvious? How long before they lost their resolve? How long before they touched . . . *kissed*?

How long?

She growled in frustration and sank under the cold water, moving her arms slowly as she glided, trying to get herself under control. Because frankly, her body was on fire.

You're a pig, you're a pig. Jeez.

Drew swam into deeper water, feeling the power of the falls as it crashed around her. She surfaced, gasping for breath. She spotted Jay floating on her back out in the sun. Again, her glance locked on her breasts and she shook her head, sinking again under water.

Pig.

But she couldn't help it. She'd been waiting for Jay to come into her life for far too many years to be patient. Her hands itched to touch her, her mouth begged for a kiss, and her body longed for the feel of Jay's pressed against her.

And she didn't know how much longer she could wait.

They didn't say another word to one another, they didn't even swim near the other, but Jay was acutely aware of where Drew was at all times. And she assumed the same was true for Drew. She could feel Drew's eyes on her.

And her body was numb from the cold water.

She glanced over her shoulder, finding Drew, still swimming in deeper water. She moved to shore, carefully stepping over the rocks to hoist herself to the edge. She pulled herself up, shivering. Her feet were bare and the smooth surface of the rocks was warm against them. Brushing her hair back from her face, she turned into the sun, feeling the moisture drying on her skin.

She heard the water splash behind her, heard Drew pull herself out. She turned slowly, watching as Drew pulled her hair together, shaking out the water before slicking it back off her face. Her body was exquisite. Her face flawless. And those eyes . . . God, she could fall in and drown there.

And it was those eyes that held her now, warming her much more than the sun could. She didn't move as Drew came closer. She wasn't even aware if she was breathing or not. She couldn't move away, she couldn't even think.

And she couldn't stop herself as she took a tiny step toward Drew, her hands reaching for Drew the same instant Drew reached for her. Their mouths met in a wild and hungry kiss. Their first kiss. Jay heard the moans coming from her throat, but she couldn't stop them. Her mouth opened, letting Drew inside, her own tongue sliding wetly across Drew's.

God, they were out in public but she didn't care, didn't

protest when Drew grabbed her hips and pulled their lower bodies together. All she could do was strain to get closer, her hands moving at will across Drew's hot body, her legs opening, gasping as Drew's strong thigh pressed against her.

The jolt that pierced her core brought her to her senses. Here they were, practically groping each other, their mouths still fused together, their moans mingling as they were within seconds of becoming very intimate in a very public place. And a part of her didn't care in the least. How could she? Not when Drew's hands were slipping up her waist, not when her nipples were so hard she didn't know if she could stand it when Drew finally touched them. And not when she felt like she was seconds away from an orgasm as Drew's thigh moved against her. But when Drew's hand closed around her breast, her fingers rubbing across her nipple, when she heard Drew's moan, she knew she had to stop.

She tore her mouth from Drew's, turned without looking and flung herself back into the cold spring water, surprised that it didn't boil as her heated body entered.

Oh, God, but did that feel good or what?

How long could they wait?

Not any longer.

CHAPTER THIRTY

Jay floated lazily in the pool, her eyes closed against the bright sun, one hand moving through the water to put her in motion again. She tried to keep her mind clear, tried not to think . . . but *damn*, that kiss.

And really, could it be called just a kiss? Had their hands not roamed each other's body? Had their breasts not been pressed together? And God, had Drew's thigh not been between her legs, separated only by a very thin—and wet—piece of cloth?

And had she not wanted to rip that piece of cloth away?

She rolled off the float and into the water, submerging in the somewhat cool water. Cool, but not nearly cold enough to douse the flames.

They'd done so well, keeping everything light between them, keeping everything in perspective. But really, did they think they could see each other every day, all day, and continue? And did she really think she could wait until things were resolved with Katherine before exploring any type of relationship with Drew?

She swam to the end of the pool, climbing the concrete steps and moving to a lounge chair in the shade. She saw Eleu approaching and was thankful. She'd rather have idle conversation with the innkeeper than be alone with her own thoughts.

"You are enjoying the pool instead of the beach today?"

Jay smiled and motioned to the chair next to her. "Yes, just relaxing after our bike ride. Why don't you join me?"

Eleu sat down, looking around the pool. "Where is your friend Drew?"

"She had a message from her work, so she needed to call in."

"It's strange not seeing you two together." Eleu leaned back in her chair. "It's none of my business, of course, but I'm slightly confused by your lodging arrangements."

Jay laughed. "That makes two of us."

"I thought you and Katherine were together."

How did she answer that? "Technically, yes. We've been together a number of years. Eight, actually." She rubbed her damp hair with her towel, then brushed it back. "But it's over. We just haven't officially ended it."

"Because of Jenna?"

"No, Jenna's not the cause. We just weren't meant to be. There are a lot of reasons. Their affair is just a sign of the end, that's all."

Eleu nodded. "My mother always told me to watch people. You learn more from their actions than their words. Katherine and Jenna, their affair is physical only. It goes no deeper than that." She smiled at Jay. "You and Drew, your affair is spiritual and very deep, although I suspect not yet physical."

Jay felt a blush creep across her face. "So if I told you Drew and I are just friends, you wouldn't believe me?"

"No, I would. Friendship is a necessity. Physical love will only take you so far. True, long-lasting love is not between two

171

people, it's between two souls."

Jay stared at Eleu, absorbing her words. "I think you may be right."

Eleu smiled and pointed to the giant cedar tree that towered next to the pool area. "Has anyone told you the legend of Okalani and her tree?"

"No."

Eleu nodded. "It started with a forbidden love. But as we know, we can't help who we fall in love with. Neither could Okalani. She was the daughter of the ruling king, you see. Her impending marriage was all arranged. She had no choice. But she had fallen in love, in love with the son of a common laborer. When the king found out, he forbid the laborer and his son to come near the palace. So, the son took to the seas, vowing to bring back the greatest treasure to his love. A year passed before he returned, and the princess had married. But the son, now a pirate, brought back riches of gold . . . and a lone sapling. The cedar tree. He presented it to his love. He said as long as the tree lives, so would their love. He said after a rain, I'll send you a sign so you'll know I am with you. And Okalani planted it here, in secret, so her father wouldn't find it. And it grew and grew. And after each rain, the rainbow would appear, circling the tree, reminding Okalani of their love. And each year, the pirate returned, asking for Okalani to join him, to leave the island, and each year she declined, bound by her duties here. Their affair lasted for years, long after Okalani had married, long after the pirate had grown gray. She bore three sons. Legend has it that all three were sons of the pirate.

"Then one year, the pirate didn't return. Okalani waited and waited. Finally, she sent her own ships out to find him, to look to the land of the cedars. Wherever he brought the cedar tree from, that's where she thought he would be. They came back time and again with other saplings, but no pirate. That's where the forest of cedars came from, from Okalani's search for her pirate. She never found him, and he never returned, yet the rainbows continued to show themselves after each rain.

"And still to this day, after a rain . . . the rainbows come."

Jay pulled her gaze from Eleu to look at the giant cedar—the rainbow cedar. "What a lovely story."

Eleu smiled. "Legend, not story. Everyone on the island learns the legend of Okalani and her tree."

"And does everyone believe it?"

Eleu laughed. "Where do you think all the trees came from?"

Jay stared at the tree. "Where's the palace?"

"Oh, the palace didn't survive. A hurricane wiped it out long, long ago. But the tree has survived many hurricanes. Some think the tree will never die."

"What do you think?"

"I think the tree brings love. As long as there is love, the tree will not die."

Jay looked past Eleu, watching as Drew walked over, her suit thankfully covered with shorts and a T-shirt. Eleu followed her gaze, her smile widening.

"See how she looks at you," she said softly. "Her soul cares for you."

Jay's breath caught at her words, her eyes locked on Drew's as she approached. They had not spoken, not really, since the kissing scene at the waterfalls. They'd dried, they'd dressed, they'd gotten on their bikes and coasted down the mountain. And then the tour group was there, and they didn't have a moment alone. And once back in the car, they'd played it safe, stopping for a quick burger for lunch, eating outdoors, surrounded by people, anything to avoid an intimate conversation. Even now, Jay hoped Eleu wouldn't disappear, wouldn't leave them alone.

"Hello, Eleu," Drew said.

Eleu smiled. "I was keeping Jay company until you returned." She stood. "Do you have a preference for dinner or do you want to wait until the others come back before you decide?"

"Actually, I got a call from Jenna." Drew glanced at Jay. "Seems the only tickets they could get were for the dinner theater. And it's over late. They won't be able to get a shuttle over."

Jay looked at Eleu who nodded. "Yes, most of the island shuttles stop early. But I am curious, if they spend so much time on Oahu, why did they secure lodging here in Maui? Why not just stay on Oahu to begin with?"

"I think at the time, Katherine was looking for something less crowded, and a little quieter than anywhere near Honolulu."

"Yes. And she did mention that she and Jenna enjoyed the museums. Unfortunately, we are more for the outdoor enthusiast here on Maui."

"Which is why we've enjoyed it so much," Drew said.

"Well then, dinner will just be the two of you. Shall I plan something special?"

Jay's eyes darted to Drew. *Something special?* They would be alone. This evening. Tonight. No Katherine. No Jenna. Just the two of them.

Oh, dear Lord.

"I was thinking we could just walk the beach to catch the sunset and stop off at that little hut that advertises the fried seafood baskets," Drew said. "How does that sound?"

Before Jay could reply, Eleu was shaking her head. "No, no, no. Fried fish, fried shrimp, fried clam, fried scallops . . . fried *everything*. There is nothing good for you there."

Drew laughed. "But we're from Texas. Fried food is a staple."

"No. I will get dinner for you. You go to the beach, watch the sunset. I will have dinner when you come back. Roasted pork with a pineapple glaze, with Asian noodles. I shall have a beautiful bottle of wine. Go, enjoy the sunset. But remember, even though some think of the setting sun as the end of the day, it is merely the end of a chapter. The moon will rise, the stars will shine, all having their own chapters, their own secrets. So go, see the sun set into the ocean, then wait for the moon to rise from that very ocean. Just another chapter. Perhaps for you too." She smiled sweetly at them. "When you return, I shall have dinner. Now go."

"I like Eleu," Drew said. "She's very lyrical. She seems older than she is."

Jay nodded. "Yes. She's probably not even our age."

They walked on in silence, heading to the west, watching the sun. But Jay suspected Drew, like herself, had little interest in the setting sun. There were too many things left unsaid.

"Are you upset that Katherine and Jenna are stuck on Oahu tonight?"

Jay shook her head. "Upset? No. Frankly, it's less stressful when they're not around. And honestly, I don't have room in my head to worry about them right now."

"Because of me?"

Jay smiled. "Because of *us*. And because I lost control today."

Drew laughed. "*We* lost control." She took Jay's hand, holding it lightly as they walked. "Are you upset that we kissed?"

"Is that what we did?" Jay squeezed her hand. "It felt like much more than a kiss."

"Should we talk about it?"

"Talk about what? We're attracted to each other. We knew it would happen eventually. But I'm not exactly single. And my girlfriend is having an affair with your date. I *know* they're having an affair but I act like I don't. And now they're stuck on another island tonight and won't even be here to chaperone us." She laughed. "God, how screwed up is all of this?"

Drew took a deep breath. "Yes, well, it is what it is. And there's not a lot we can do about any of it." She stopped walking. "So I think we should just take it in stride, try to make it as normal as possible, and *enjoy* ourselves. Despite everything, I love being here with you, doing things with you, just being with you. I mean snorkeling, swimming, all of it. I enjoy *you*."

"You make it all seem so simple."

"It's only complicated if we allow it to be. Like now, we're standing on this beautiful beach, watching another awesome sunset. Just the two of us. Let's stop there. We're watching a sunset. That's all. Then we'll walk back and maybe I'll try to steal a kiss," she said with a laugh. "And you'll stop me because someone might be watching. Then Eleu will have dinner for us. And then afterward . . ."

Jay tugged her hand, bringing her closer. "Then afterward what?" she asked quietly.

Drew took a step back and shook her head. "No, no, no. If you want me to behave, don't tempt me. Because I *will* kiss you right here on the beach regardless of who might be watching." She leaned closer. "Have you already forgotten what happened earlier today?"

Jay tilted her head back, her frustration growing. "You're right. I forgot we have zero control." She forced a smile to her face. "I wish we were home."

"Home? Austin?"

Jay turned, retracing their steps back to the cottages. "Yeah. I want this all to be over with. This charade we're forced to play."

Drew fell into step beside her. "Are we being forced? Or are we doing it willingly?"

"Well, now how wonderfully blissful would the next five days be if I called her on it? We have a huge fight, all dramatic and everything, and you and Jenna get to witness it, along with most likely Eleu and anyone else within earshot." Jay laughed. "Because let me tell you, Katherine *hates* to be accused of anything, and she turns mean and defensive in the blink of an eye. And being the talented attorney that she is, she'll have it twisted and turned around in no time, and *I'll* be the one to blame, *I'll* be the bad guy in all this, not her. And *I'll* have ruined the vacation for everyone."

"She hates to lose, huh?"

"See, if she ends things on her terms, she's still the winner. She won't let me end things, be the one to leave. It'll look like she's a failure and she'll never let that happen. So no matter how it ends, she'll make sure that it's my fault. But I'm prepared for that, and honestly, I don't really care." She stopped and spun around. "But *damn*, I can't believe they have the nerve to miss the last shuttle flight. That's what pisses me off. It's like she's *daring* me to suspect an affair, *daring* me to say something."

Drew shrugged. "So do it. You'll only ruin the vacation for Katherine and Jenna. You could never ruin it for me."

"What? Just say *fuck* it?"

Drew's eyebrows shot up, then she laughed. "I do believe that's the first time I've heard such language from you."

Jay grabbed her hand and started walking again. "I swear, I could cuss like a sailor if I didn't stop myself. Because, you know, sometimes situations just require a good cuss word."

They walked in silence—their hands still clasped—toward the lights of the cottages. The garden and pool area was alive with activity as Eleu provided dinner for the guests, although there were still a few enjoying a late swim. Or perhaps they were enjoying the concoctions Carlos created for them.

By unspoken consent, they stayed in the shadows, keeping to the trees as they moved around the garden. It was nice holding hands. And Jay wasn't ready for it to end.

"I like being with you," she said softly. "Like this." She squeezed Drew's hand. "I think it's romantic."

"What? Holding hands?"

"Yes. It has an intimacy all its own. Much like kissing." She slowed her steps. "I like to kiss."

"Do you now?"

Jay smiled. "I do." She stopped, finding them next to the giant cedar tree, their shadows mixing with those of the trees around them. "Eleu told me the legend of the tree." She released

Drew's hand, moving closer to rub her hand across its bark, so different from the small cedars she was used to back home. "Okalani fell in love with a soon-to-be pirate, but being the daughter of the king, she was promised to another. The pirate left, vowing to return with riches for her. He brought back gold . . . and this young cedar tree." She turned to Drew. "I'm probably telling the story all wrong. Eleu told it almost like a fairy-tale."

"Go on. Finish the story."

"Well, the pirate told Okalani to plant the tree. He told her as long as the tree was alive, so would their love be. He told her there would be a sign each time it rained, to remind her of his love."

"The rainbow?"

Jay nodded. "He came back every year asking her to join him, but she never would. And then one year he stopped coming. Eleu said she sent out ships to find him, but all they ever brought back were more young saplings, much like the cedar he'd brought her. She planted them all," she said, waving her hands around them to the trees. "And even though they never saw each other again, the tree continued to grow, and the rainbows still came after every rain." The shadows were darker now but Jay could still make out Drew's face, could still see the expression in her eyes. "I think it's a sweet story," she whispered.

Drew stared at her. "I'm in love with you, you know."

Yes. Jay knew that, didn't she? Couldn't she see it in Drew's eyes every time she looked at her? She wondered if hers revealed the same. "Yes." Just one simple word, yet she saw Drew's breath leave her.

The sounds around them—the splashing of the pool, the quiet conversations over dinner, the gentle rustle of the trees in the wind—disappeared as Drew reached for her, cupping her face, bringing her lips closer. Their kiss this time was soft, quiet . . . missing the fire and explosion of their first out by the waterfall.

A tiny moan escaped as Jay's hands slipped around Drew's waist, pulling her near, sliding one hand under her shirt and against her flesh. She felt Drew tremble at her touch and her mouth opened, their kisses turning hungry as their bodies melded. She felt the hardness of the tree against her back as Drew held her there, and she moaned again, her body taking on a life of its own as it strained to get closer.

"Jay, we should stop," Drew said against her lips before moving her mouth lower, gently nibbling at the hollow of her throat.

"We shouldn't have started," Jay breathed, turning her head to expose more of her neck to Drew's lips, loving the feel as they moved against her skin. Her breath came faster as she lost herself in Drew's kisses. Yes, they should stop. But it was the furthest thing from her mind as her hand glided up Drew's side, brushing her fingertips across her ribs. She was so close. She could feel the swell of Drew's breast. So close.

"We've got to stop, Jay," Drew said again before finding Jay's mouth, kissing her hard. "Don't you dare touch me," she said.

Jay moaned, her tongue doing battle with Drew's as her legs parted, letting Drew nearer, feeling her thigh slip between her legs. Yes, they should stop. They were but a stone's throw from the garden. One of the other guests could walk upon them at any moment. None of that mattered. "No, it's too late to stop," Jay murmured, bringing Drew's mouth back to her own, pressing her hot center hard against Drew's thigh. She slipped both hands under Drew's shirt now, sliding them around her waist, her thumbs dangerously close to her breasts.

"God, you're killing me," Drew breathed as she grasped Jay's hips, pulling her intimately against her own. "I want you so much."

Jay lifted her head, trying to see Drew's eyes in the shadows. "I know I said we should wait. I know I said I didn't want to be like them, but I swear I'm going to *die* if I don't touch you." She didn't wait for Drew's response. She couldn't. Her hands moved, covering Drew's breast, loving the sounds that came from Drew's mouth, hating the fabric that stood in her way. Impatiently, she shoved the bikini top higher, finally feeling the warm, soft flesh of Drew's breasts, feeling her nipples harden and press into her palms. She closed her eyes, her head leaning back against the tree as her fingers teased the pebbled skin.

"*Jay*—"

"*Yes* . . . yes, I'm in love with you too." The low, guttural sound Drew uttered made her squeeze Drew's breasts harder. "Touch me," she whispered. "Please . . . touch me."

"*Jay?*"

Jay left Drew's breast, finding her hand and shoving it between the waistband of her shorts and her skin. "Please . . . touch me," she whispered again, her hips already undulating, rocking slowly against Drew.

She felt Drew hesitate only for a second, then her hand moved, sliding across her hot flesh, slipping easily past the thin material of the bikini bottom she still wore. Her eyes slammed shut as her legs parted further, her mouth buried against Drew's neck, stifling her moan as she felt Drew's fingers brush against her, teasing her. Her hips rocked, urging Drew closer, begging for her touch.

Then Drew's fingers were there, moving through her wetness and slipping inside her in one motion. "God, you're so wet," she moaned. "Don't make me stop now, Jay."

Stop? No, it would have been easier to scale to the top of this tree than to make Drew stop. She bit down hard against Drew's neck, her hips moving forcefully against Drew's fingers, taking her inside, then letting her slip away, only to come back inside her again, harder and harder, faster and faster, until Jay felt her hips slamming against Drew. She was panting, unable to stop, and long past caring if someone could hear them. It had been too many years since she'd felt this primal hunger, too many years since she'd lost control.

And lose control she did as Drew's fingers slipped from within her, finding her swollen clit, stroking her, matching the rhythm of her hips. Her body exploded in an instant. There was no time to prepare, and it took all of her willpower not to scream out at the top of her lungs. But Drew's mouth was there, catching the sounds, holding her close to her body as her tremors subsided.

And it was then she finally came to her senses. She shook her head, trying to stifle the laughter that threatened to bubble out. But she couldn't. She buried her face against Drew, laughing quietly.

"Oh, my God." She laughed. "I can't believe we just did that."

"Neither can I."

Jay pulled back, her face still flushed. "It was fantastic. But do you think anyone heard us?" Drew laughed out loud and Jay quickly covered Drew's mouth with her hand. "Shhh. Quiet." Which brought more laughter as they finally pulled away from each other.

"There you are," Eleu said from the shadows. "I thought I heard your voices."

"Oh, God, just shoot me now," Jay told Drew, feeling her face turn yet another shade of red as she straightened her clothes.

"Whenever you are ready, I have dinner for you."

"Thanks, Eleu," Drew said. "We're starving."

"Yes. I'm sure you are. I trust your sunset walk was satisfactory then?"

"It was the best yet."

"Excellent. Come with me. The night is still young."

They followed her along the path back to the garden where the shadows disappeared. Jay glanced at Drew, trying to read her expression. But when Drew met her eyes, everything was there for Jay to see. She didn't try to hide. And Jay couldn't stop herself from moving closer, from slipping her hand inside Drew's arm, grasping her elbow as they walked. She just needed the contact.

But when they got to the garden, their normal table was empty. Jay raised a questioning eyebrow at Eleu.

"I thought perhaps you might enjoy dinner inside tonight," she said with a coy smile. "I took the liberty of arranging the table in Drew's cottage. I hope that's okay."

As their eyes met, Eleu's knowing look made Jay feel exposed. And embarrassed. But Eleu smiled slightly, her own eyes questioning.

Jay finally nodded. "I think that's an excellent idea." She turned to Drew. "Okay?"

"Yes, that's fine with me."

Eleu smiled at them both. "Wonderful. I picked out a special bottle of wine for you. If there is anything else you need for this evening, just let me know."

"Thank you, Eleu."

"My pleasure. Enjoy."

When she was gone, Drew smiled at Jay. "Why do I get the impression she knows far more than she should?"

Jay linked arms with Drew and led her out of the garden. "We had a chat this afternoon. She's very wise for someone her age."

"Wise, yes, but I think she enjoys playing matchmaker."

"I think you may be right."

And when Drew opened the door to her cottage, Jay's breath caught. Eleu had set a perfect table, with candles illuminating the white cloth. The windows were opened, the ocean breeze lifting the curtains, making the flames dance in the room. Through the door to the bedroom, a lamp was on, the comforter pulled back invitingly across the bed.

Jay turned to Drew. "Oh, God, we're in trouble."

"I think it's too late for that." Drew closed the door, closing out the world. She glanced to the table, then back to Jay. "I'm not really hungry right now."

Jay shook her head. "Me, either." She moved closer. There was no use trying to prolong the inevitable. Not after what had just happened at the tree. "Not for food, anyway."

And there was no rush this time as they moved into each other's arms, hands sliding under shirts, touching warm flesh, mouths meeting in a slow, tender kiss.

"I love kissing you," Jay said, moving against Drew's lips. "Kissing you, touching you."

Drew's mouth moved across her skin, her breath whispering into her ear. "I've dreamed of making love to you for so long. I can't believe how nervous I am."

"I'm guessing your dreams didn't include up against a tree with a potential audience within feet of us." Jay slid her hands up, cupping Drew's breasts again. "Don't be nervous. I just want it to be normal. I want to make love with you, sleep with you, wake up with you. And make love all over again." She moved her hands, feeling Drew's nipples hard against her palms. "And God, I want my mouth on you," she said as she found Drew's lips again.

She wasn't sure how—or when—they got to the bedroom, but she didn't hesitate as she pulled Drew's shirt over her head. The tiny red bikini top, she nearly ripped off, finally exposing Drew's breasts to her greedy eyes. She slowly raised her gaze, meeting Drew's. "I just now realized how many times I envisioned you naked." She smiled, embarrassed by her admission. "I'm afraid I didn't do you justice."

Drew reached out and took her hand, bringing it to her body. She pressed Jay's hand against her breast, a soft moan drifting through the room.

Jay moved closer, both hands covering Drew's breasts before dipping her head, her lips replacing fingers, her tongue swirling against a taut nipple. She was surprised at the softness, surprised at the tiny gasps coming from Drew at her touch. She lifted her head, her mouth moving slowly up Drew's body, loving the taste of her skin, her tongue slipping again into Drew's hot mouth. She lost herself in their kisses, their tongues moving wetly against the other, their hands roving idly against flesh.

Then Drew pulled away, her breathing labored, her eyes dark with desire. "Take this off," she gasped, tugging at Jay's shirt. But Jay's bikini top proved more elusive, and they were soon giggling as it became a twisted mess around her. "My God, does it have a lock or something?" Drew muttered. Jay raised her arms, letting Drew pull it over her head. "Oh, my," she breathed, staring at Jay. "Beautiful."

But Jay stopped her exploration, her hands going to Drew's waist, slipping inside her shorts and urging them down. She wasn't sure how much longer she could stand. She wanted to be naked, she wanted to be on the bed, and God, she wanted Drew's weight on top of her. "Hurry."

And Drew did, stripping them both naked in a matter of seconds, then guiding Jay to the bed. But it was Jay's weight which settled over Drew, Jay who pushed Drew's thighs apart with her knee, and Jay whose mouth claimed Drew's breast possessively. Never aggressive in bed, she wasn't sure what came over her, but her need to hold Drew—to kiss her, to touch her, to make love to her—was overwhelming.

She pulled her mouth from Drew's breast, "The words *I want you* don't seem to express everything I'm feeling right now." She dipped her head again, her tongue raking across a nipple, feeling it harden even more. "But *God*, I want you."

She felt Drew's thighs move under her, and she burrowed between her legs, her hips moving slowly, grinding against Drew. Drew grasped her waist, holding her close as she opened up for her. Jay could feel the slick wetness against her stomach, could feel the hardness of her own clit as she rocked against Drew. She wanted to be inside her, wanted to feel her wetness against her fingers, and so she slipped her hand between them, never losing the rhythm they'd set.

"God, *yes*," Drew hissed, arching up to meet her, opening as Jay's fingers thrust into her.

She was so wet, like silk between her fingers, but it wasn't enough . . . Jay couldn't get nearly close enough. She wanted *all* of her. She withdrew her fingers, hearing the frustration as Drew groaned at their lack of contact. Jay covered her mouth with her own, then moved lower, her lips closing around a nipple, sucking it hard into her mouth, feeling Drew's hips begin to move again as she suckled her breast.

"Please, Jay," she whimpered, reaching for Jay's hand, trying to move it between her thighs again.

"Yes. But I want you to come in my mouth," she whispered, leaving her breast, her mouth moving wetly across her skin. "I want to taste you. I want my tongue inside you." She raised her head again. "I want to make you come with my mouth." She cupped Drew's hips, urging her legs apart. In the soft glow of the lamp, she saw the glistening wetness that waited for her, felt Drew writhe beneath her.

"*Please*," Drew whimpered again. "Love me. *Please.*"

Jay's breath caught at that simple word, hearing all it conveyed. At that moment, she realized what Drew was offering her, and what gift she was about to give to Drew. At that moment, she realized how deeply she had fallen in love with her—her body, her mind . . . and her soul.

"*Yes.* I'm going to love you."

She closed her eyes, accepting the gift, letting her mouth cover Drew, her tongue sliding through her wetness, slipping deep inside her as she held Drew. She moaned, savoring her taste, memorizing the feel of Drew against her mouth. Her tongue snaked out, finding Drew's clit, teasing her before sucking it into her mouth. Drew's hips bucked, pressing hard against her face and she held her tightly, her tongue moving with lightning speed as Drew gasped, her hands tangled in Jay's hair, holding her steady.

She felt Drew's orgasm build, felt Drew swell against her mouth, felt the throbbing ache between Drew's thighs. Drew's short gasps came quickly now, her hips moving wildly against Jay's mouth. Jay held on tight, at the last instant, her lips closing around Drew's clit, sucking it hard as Drew screamed out, her mouth flooded with Drew's wetness as she rocked against her.

"*Jesus*, that was . . ." She lay spent, her legs still parted, Jay still nestled between them.

At last, Jay's mouth released her, her tongue moving deliberately now, caressing, her lips moving leisurely as she slid back up her body, pausing at her breasts again.

She finally lifted her head, meeting Drew's eyes. "I love you."

CHAPTER THIRTY-ONE

Drew moved under the covers, stretching her legs out, trying not to wake Jay. They were still tangled together, much as they'd been all night. She couldn't even begin to count the number of times they'd drifted off to sleep, only to wake, to touch, to make love again.

At midnight, they'd remembered dinner . . . and the wine. But neither did little more than pick at the food. They couldn't seem to keep their eyes—or their hands—off each other. So, dinner was left largely uneaten, and the wine bottle, which was now empty, sat beside the bed.

"What are you thinking?"

Drew smiled, turning her head. "Not thinking really. Just kinda . . . remembering."

Jay stretched, her legs moving against Drew's, then rolled to her side, facing Drew. She yawned once, then laughed. "I'm exhausted. I'm sore. And I'm so totally happy right now."

Drew rolled over too, moving her hand lazily under the covers, feeling the smooth skin over Jay's hip. Her hands—and her mouth—had explored every inch of Jay last night, and she wanted to do it all over again.

"I really wish I'd met you years ago," Jay said.

But Drew shook her head. "No. Because years ago, you weren't where you are now. In your relationship, I mean. You wouldn't have given me a second glance."

"I don't believe that's true. Had we met two, three, four, even six years ago, I think I still would have fallen in love with you. I look in your eyes and I . . . I see *something*. I can't really explain it. But I . . . I feel like I belong, if that makes sense. With Katherine, there was always that edge, that wall, which I never crossed. There was always a barrier, it seemed like."

"Maybe because you felt like you couldn't be you. Or maybe you didn't feel like you were good enough, could measure up to her."

Jay nodded. "Maybe. Or maybe I just could never see her soul, you know. I meant that when I said your eyes were like a book to me. You don't ever try to hide anything from me, do you?"

Drew leaned closer, touching Jay's lips lightly with her own. "Should I?"

"No. I like you open like this." She smiled. "Saves me having to guess what you're thinking."

Drew's hand moved higher, cupping Jay's small breast, feeling her nipple harden beneath her palm. Even now, as sated as they were, she heard the tiny gasp Jay uttered, could feel her heartbeat quicken its pace. She sighed. "Yes, I wish we'd met years ago." Her gaze locked with Jay's. "Because I love you. And it seems like it's been so many wasted years."

"I know."

Drew sighed again, rolling away from Jay and onto her back.

"But it is what it is." And in reality, nothing had really changed. Jay was still not a free woman. And what they'd done last night amounted to little more than an affair. Because in the light of day, they were just *friends*. Katherine and Jenna would return today and they would continue to play this charade they'd begun weeks and weeks ago.

"Drew?"

"Hmm?"

"Do you think—?" But a pounding on the back door stopped her in mid-sentence. They looked at each other. "Oh, God, please say it's not them already."

"Drew? Jay? It's Eleu. Please open the door."

"Thank God," Jay said with relief. "We're not exactly dressed for a confrontation with Katherine and Jenna."

Drew pulled on her shorts but couldn't find the T-shirt they'd discarded last night. She did, however, find Jay's black bikini top, still a twisted mess. She tossed it to her with a smile. "Have you seen my shirt?"

"Drew?" Eleu called again from outside.

"Coming." She opened the closet and pulled out her bag, finding a clean shirt to slip on before opening the door. She greeted Eleu with a smile, not certain whether she should feel embarrassed or not to have Jay in her bed. But then she remembered the romantic dinner Eleu had left for them and decided she would be embarrassed if Jay *weren't* in her bed. "Good morning."

"Yes, yes. I'm sure it is. But it must come to an end." She looked around Drew and into the room. "Jay?"

"Yes. I'm sure you already know she's here."

Eleu laughed. "I had hoped, yes. But it is time. Katherine called. They are on the first shuttle of the morning. They will be here in time for breakfast."

Drew frowned. "How long?"

"Half hour, forty-five minutes. But we have time. Tell Jay to come, please. We must make your cottage presentable."

Drew ran her hands through her hair and sighed. "Great way to start the morning."

"It will be fine. And after the rooms are fixed, you two will take an early swim to clear your heads, even on a morning like today when there is rain in the air. Then you shall be ready for breakfast with the others. Come, we must not waste time."

Drew nodded. "I'll get Jay."

"I will begin clearing dinner."

Drew went back into the bedroom and closed the door, finding Jay already dressed. "You heard?"

"Yes. And an early morning swim sounds great." Jay came closer, moving into Drew's arms. "Because we need to talk."

Drew's arms tightened around her. Talk? What was there to talk about? She closed her eyes, feeling Jay's lips move across her face.

"Meet you out front?"

Drew nodded, watching Jay slip from the room.

"How does this look?" Eleu asked after she'd rumpled the sheets and comforter on Katherine's bed. She bent, pounding one of the pillows into shape. "Good?"

Jay nodded. "Yes. It'll work. But what about Drew's?"

"Milkea is there. She will change the sheets and pull out the sleeper sofa as Drew normally does. It will be fine."

Jay spun around. "Will it? Why are we doing this, Eleu? She and Jenna go off together, stay out all night. There are no questions from us. They're not even trying to hide it. Why the hell should we?"

Eleu came closer, grasping Jay's hands. "Because you are not them. And because you still care about other people's feelings. So we do this to keep peace." She smiled. "That is true, isn't it?"

"Yes, it's true." Jay laughed. "But I think it's just because you don't want to have a scene here and have your other guests talking about us."

"That is also true." Eleu released her hands. "Now, you will have your coffee like normal. And then you will both disappear, coming back just in time for breakfast. Yes?"

Jay nodded. "But it looks like rain."

"Yes. We had rain during the night. But you must go. If you stay here waiting, you will only feel guilty."

Jay shook her head. "No, I don't feel guilty. Not at all. But if I had to guess, I'd say you've done this sort of thing before."

Eleu laughed, a delightful sound on an otherwise dreary morning. "I have only done this once before. And surprisingly, it was also with two female couples."

Drew waited under a palm tree, watching for Jay. Amazingly, her cottage had been transformed in a matter of minutes: the bedroom tidied, sheets changed, sleeper sofa pulled open and made, then the sheets intentionally rumpled. She'd even had time for a shower.

And like Jay had said, she was exhausted, she was sore . . . and she was as happy as she could remember being in many, many years. Happy. Yet sad.

Sad because, while nothing had really changed, everything had changed. How were they going to be able to sit down to breakfast with Katherine and Jenna and pretend they weren't now lovers? Pretend to keep their eyes off each other? And pretend they weren't dying to be alone? And sad because tonight, Jay would retire to her cottage with Katherine, would crawl into bed with Katherine, and would wake with her. And Drew? She'd be on her lumpy sofa, *aching* to have Jay beside her. And yet another day would pass.

And it would be another day wasted.

"Hey you."

She turned, pushing her thoughts away as Jay walked through

the sand, a smile on her face.

"All fixed up?"

Jay nodded. "Eleu is amazing." She wrapped her fingers around Drew's arm. "I'm sorry our morning had to come to such an abrupt end."

Drew shrugged. "I guess we should be thankful Katherine called."

"She only called so that Eleu could have breakfast waiting for them. Don't you think it's strange she called Eleu and not us?" Jay took her hand and pulled her toward the beach. "But I don't want to talk about Katherine. I don't even want to *think* about Katherine."

They walked to the water's edge, their bare feet sinking into the damp sand as they stood looking out over the ocean. It was still overcast, the air cooler than it had been, the sun hiding behind clouds, the waves and wind a little stronger than they'd seen.

"Last night was fantastic," Drew said quietly, the wind carrying her words away.

Jay nodded. "Yes. It was beyond fantastic." She sighed. "And now they're back."

"We didn't really have time to consider anything, did we?"

"No, we didn't. But I don't regret it. Do you?"

"Are you kidding? It was the best night of my life."

"But now?" Jay asked, looking at Drew. "You look so sad."

"Do I?" Drew turned away, beginning to walk again. "Yeah, I guess I am," she said.

Jay touched her arm, stopping her. "Nothing about this is perfect," she said. "But like you said earlier . . . it is what it is."

"Yes. It's just funny. A few days ago, you were the one saying you didn't want an affair with me. And now, I guess, it's me. I don't want an affair with you, Jay. But it seems that's what we have."

"No. That's not what we have. What we shared last night can't ever be called an affair. I fell in love with you weeks ago.

Last night was inevitable. We both knew that."

"And I'm being selfish. I just want us to be alone, to be able to be ourselves. And I knew coming in that wouldn't be the case."

Jay turned into the wind, her hair lifting around her face. "I'm not sure what I thought would happen. I guess I thought maybe we could ignore this . . . this *thing* between us until we got back home. I know that's crazy now." She glanced at Drew. "I mean, we've spent every day together, just us. There wasn't any defense anymore. We made love." She moved in front of Drew, standing close. "We made love last night. And I've never felt closer to anyone than I did you. It was so . . . so powerful being with you like that."

"I'm totally in love with you, Jay. And I'm scared you're going to break my heart," she said. "Scared to death."

Jay shook her head. "No." She moved into Drew's arms and Drew held her tight. "No, I'm not going to break your heart," she whispered into Drew's ear. "I'm going to love you to death." Her lips lingered before she pulled away and slipped out of her arms again.

"So now what? We go back and keep on pretending?"

Jay took a deep breath and squared her shoulders. "No." She shook her head. "I'm tired of playing games. Aren't you?"

"So you're ready for that confrontation with her?"

"I'm ready for the truth. I'm ready to get on with my life."

But the relief Drew felt at those words was short-lived. When they returned to the garden, Jenna and Katherine were already there, sipping strong Hawaiian coffee and chatting with Eleu.

"There you two are," Katherine said with a smile. "I was hoping you'd be here waiting for me, Jay."

"Waiting for you?"

"Yes. I missed you terribly last night." Her smile was beaming and Drew frowned. Something was up.

"But I trust you enjoyed the theater and dinner," Jay said as she pulled out a chair.

"Oh, it was fun, but I hated that we missed the last shuttle."

"Well, we managed without you."

"Something special for breakfast?" Eleu asked quietly behind Jay. "Or just fruit?"

"This is fine, Eleu. Don't go to any trouble."

"For you, Drew?"

"I'm good, thanks." Drew pulled out a chair opposite Jay, chancing a quick glance her way. Jay looked at her and Drew saw a quiet determination on her face.

"I hope you guys didn't have any excursions planned today," Jenna said. "I think we'd like to join you at the beach, just hang out, you know."

"No, actually we didn't make any plans for today," Drew said. "Although it still looks like it could rain."

"Eleu says the clouds will burn off by noon," Katherine said. She turned to Jay. "I'm ready to see you in that cute black bikini," she added with a wink.

Drew's eyebrows shot up. Was that the same black bikini that was a tangled mess after Drew had ripped it from Jay's body last night?

"You hate the ocean, remember," Jay said as she stabbed a piece of pineapple.

"I didn't say I wanted to get in the water." She put her coffee cup down, smiling at Jay. "It'll be good to spend the day with you though."

"Will it?"

"Of course." She stared at Jay. "But you seem a little agitated this morning. What is it? Are you angry that we missed the shuttle last night?"

Jay tilted her head as she stared at Katherine, then she flashed a quick smile. "Honestly, Kath, I didn't even know you were gone."

Drew and Jenna watched the exchange silently. Drew wondered if they were about to witness that big dramatic scene Jay had warned her about. But no, Katherine didn't even seem fazed by Jay's comment.

"Now I know that's not true." She reached across the table and touched Jay's hand, rubbing it lightly. "I'll make it up to you, darling." She glanced at Drew. "You don't mind if I steal Jay away from you today, do you? We've got some catching up to do."

Drew wasn't certain if that statement needed an answer or not, but Jay saved her from replying.

"Kath, why don't we go to our cottage?"

Katherine flashed a beaming smile, her eyes sparkling. "Excellent idea." She glanced at Jenna and winked.

Jay stood, her glance moving to Drew. There was a look there Drew wasn't sure she'd seen before. Not anger really, something even deeper than that. She watched them go, feeling jealousy rear its ugly head as Katherine's hand slipped around Jay's waist.

"That was a little odd, wasn't it?" Jenna said.

Drew nodded. "This whole trip's been odd."

Jenna sighed. "Oh, well, I suppose things will be getting back to normal."

"What do you mean?"

Jenna waved her hand dismissively. "Oh, me and Katherine. That's over with."

Drew frowned. "I thought you were in love."

"We had our fling, but we realized last night that there just wasn't anything there except lust. The sex was great. In fact, the best I've ever had. But beyond that, we really didn't enjoy each other's company all that much."

Drew felt her chest tighten at her words. Their affair was over. Now what? Was that why Katherine had been so sickeningly sweet to Jay this morning?

"I'm in the mood for a Bloody Mary," Jenna said. "Want one?"

"That'll be a good start," she said, her glance going to the cottages, wondering what was happening inside.

CHAPTER THIRTY-TWO

"We need to talk, Katherine." Jay stood at the window, looking out at the ocean. The cool breeze felt good on her heated face. "Don't you think we need to talk?"

"Does that mean you did miss me after all?"

Jay turned, ignoring the smile Katherine was offering her. "It's been a very strange trip, Kath. Even you have to admit that."

"Why do you say so?"

"Because it's almost like we're on two separate vacations, we just happen to be sharing a cottage at night."

"Oh, Jay, come on. You must admit you'd have been bored silly touring museums and galleries with me. And I'd never have done all that snorkeling and other stuff with you," she said, moving closer. "But, I've got it out of my system. I've seen my last show, toured my last museum. Now I'm ready for a little *us* time."

"Us time? Now *you're* ready?" Jay took a step back as Katherine reached for her. "It's not always about you, Kath. You still don't have a clue, do you?"

"Apparently not. But I don't care to stand here in the middle of our room talking about it." She paused. "How about a drive?"

"A drive?"

"You said you wanted to talk. Let's get alone and talk."

Jay hesitated. A drive would be good. There would be no interruptions, at least. But something told her to say what she had to say now, to get it over with. Because honestly, she didn't trust Katherine.

"Come on, Jay. If we need, we can talk over lunch somewhere."

Jay gave in. Perhaps it would be a little more civilized than having a break-up fight here in the cottage, within earshot of anyone who might pass by. "Okay. Let's take a drive."

"Wonderful. Eleu says a trip across the island is a must. How about we head to the west side?"

"What do you think is up with that?" Drew asked, motioning from their spot by the pool. Jay and Katherine were walking down the path, heading to the parking lot.

"Oh, Katherine had planned on kidnapping Jay for the afternoon. I guess they're heading out."

Drew's hand visibly shook as she set her Blood Mary down. "Kidnap?"

"She thinks Jay may be a little miffed at her, so she's booked a room at some fancy hotel on the other side of the island. She plans on wooing her." Jenna smirked. "Her words, not mine."

Drew couldn't believe that Jay would just up and leave without saying a word to her. And couldn't believe that Jay would actually *go* with Katherine. She'd thought, well, she'd thought that she and Jay had something, thought it was *real* between them.

But she'd known all along, hadn't she? Known that Jay was not free, known that Jay was still in a relationship—an eight-year relationship.

Images from last night flashed back to her—Jay's mouth leaving her breast, Jay's hand sliding across her skin, Jay's eyes locked on her own as she came, Jay's mouth moving between her legs for the third, and then fourth time. She closed her eyes, remembering. Yeah. No matter what happens, it *was* very real between them last night. As real as making love can get.

She sat up quickly. "I need to speak with Eleu."

"Well, wait a minute. Do you want to do something today?"

Drew shrugged. "Sure. Whatever you want."

"I was thinking maybe an island cruise, one of those dinner cruises where you catch the sunset. How about that?"

"Sure. It'll be romantic."

"A hotel?"

"Why not?"

Katherine got out and slammed the door, leaving Jay to follow. She stared at the multi-floored towers, then back to the retreating back of Katherine, wondering what she was up to. Especially after the nearly silent drive over. They'd made only casual conversation, nothing personal, but even that was strained.

"Great. Just great," she murmured, hurrying to catch up with Katherine. "Are you going to tell me what we're doing here?"

"How about lunch? They're supposed to have a fantastic view from the outdoor patio."

"Lunch. Okay, sure." Jay glanced at her watch. It wasn't even ten o'clock. But she dutifully followed Katherine, expecting her to lead them through the lobby. Instead, she walked to the desk, handing the clerk a credit card.

"Katherine Patton. I have reservations."

"You *what*?" Jay gasped.

Katherine turned, her smile nearly blinding. "Yes, darling. A room."

"We don't need a room, Kath," Jay said quietly, not wanting to cause a scene.

"Of course we do. We may decide to order room service," she said, winking at the clerk.

A quick blush colored Jay's face and she turned away, fuming. *Of all the nerve! Of all the fucking nerve!*

"No, I don't know where they went."

Drew paced, hating the jealousy, hating the uncertainty. "But you're sure they left?"

Eleu nodded. "Yes. Katherine drove them away."

"Well, goddamn," she mumbled. She looked at Eleu. "You think maybe, well, maybe I was wrong about Jay?" Drew shrugged. "Maybe I pushed too much."

"You were not wrong. You must have faith, Drew. Don't assume something just because it appears she has left. You don't know the circumstances."

"Yeah, but she could have at least *said* something to me."

Eleu smiled. "Jealousy is such an evil thing, isn't it? And no matter our age, it still attacks us."

Drew laughed. "You think I'm being silly?"

"Yes. I have seen how Jay looks at you. I have seen how you look at her. You must have faith. Because Okalani has blessed you."

Drew frowned.

"The garden has ears . . . and eyes."

"Oh, dear God. You *saw* us?"

Eleu nodded. "I saw love. That is all. Now, go with Jenna. Get away. It will do you no good to sit here waiting. It will only drive you crazy."

"You're right." Drew turned, finding Jenna still sitting by the pool, sipping on her drink. "She wants to do an island cruise, one of those that serve dinner."

"They're very nice. You should go."

"I guess we will." Drew nodded slightly at Eleu. "Thanks. I feel better."

CHAPTER THIRTY-THREE

Jay stood on the balcony staring out over the ocean, listening—but not really hearing—as Katherine ordered them champagne. The view was spectacular up this high. Drew would love it.

She shook her head. No, Drew would hate it. It couldn't match the grandeur of their views from the volcano. Not the views, not the smell, not the fresh air . . . and certainly not the company.

Taking a deep breath, she turned around, going back inside. The suite was huge. She could only guess what Katherine had paid for it.

"Champagne will be right up."

"Why champagne, Kath?"

"Why not?"

Jay spread her arms out. "Oh, I don't know. First of all, what the hell are we doing here? I just wanted to talk. We *need* to talk, Kath."

Katherine sat down on the sofa and crossed her legs, swinging one nonchalantly as she smiled at Jay. "Okay. So talk. What's on your mind?"

Jay hated the smile, hated the pose on the sofa, and she hated the fact that she was intimidated by Katherine. She crossed her arms defensively, wondering how to begin.

"Why are we in a two hundred dollar a night room?"

Katherine laughed. "Try two-fifty. And why not? Is it just terrible of me to want to spend some time with you? Is it so wrong to take you away so we can be alone?"

"Alone? What is it, Kath? Has Jenna run her course already?"

Katherine sat up straighter. "What are you insinuating?"

"Oh, come on. You know what I'm insinuating."

Katherine laughed. "Are you actually jealous of the time I spent with Jenna?"

Jay shook her head. "Surprisingly, jealous was not ever one of the emotions I felt. I think I just now realized that. But anger, yes. Betrayal, that too."

"*Betrayal?*"

Jay turned, staring out at the water again, trying to find its peace. Inner turmoil was a terrible thing. Part of her wanted to lash out at Katherine, to hurt her. Another part simply wished it was over with, wished she could just go home and . . . and what? All she wanted was a little happiness, a little love, a little peace and contentment. Things she realized she hadn't ever had with Katherine. Not really. Things she imagined she *could* have with Drew.

She turned back around, not afraid to meet Katherine's eyes head on. "Did you think I wouldn't notice? Do you actually think I'm that stupid to not know? And then this?" she asked, looking around the room. "You brought me here so you could have sex with me now?"

"What are you talking about?"

"Oh, stop playing games, Katherine. I'm so tired of games." She moved closer. "I'm talking about you and Jenna and your affair. That's all I'm talking about."

Katherine's eyes widened as if in shock. "How *dare* you accuse me of such a thing? I have *never* given you cause to think I would do something like that."

"How dare *you* insult me by lying about it?"

Katherine stood quickly, facing Jay. "I should be the one insulted. I'm the one being accused of *cheating* on you." She smirked. "What is it, Jay? Feeling insecure? Just because we missed the shuttle and had to stay over last night, you let your imagination get the best of you?"

"Last night? Kath, last night has nothing to do with it. We— you and I—haven't been a real couple in so long, I can't even remember. Because you're never home. Ever. And the last time we attempted to have sex, you fell asleep in the middle of it. So when Jenna comes into your life, when you make time for her like you never could for me, of course I'm going to think something is up. But this trip just confirmed it. I'm not blind to the looks between you. So don't lie to me."

"You've got it all figured out, don't you?" She laughed. "Do you think there's a reason I didn't come home, Jay? Did it ever occur to you that maybe it was because *you* were there?" She took a step closer. "Living with you had become unbearable. It was like living in an icebox."

"You're right. Your house is very cold. There's no warmth there. I know now there wasn't any love there either. I don't think you're capable of love. You're too selfish."

The blow came so quickly, Jay had no time to react. Her head snapped to the side, her cheek stinging from the force of Katherine's slap. Shocked, she stared at Katherine. "Do you feel better now? Does hitting me make you feel like you're in control?"

Katherine slapped her again, causing her to stumble backward. This time, she tasted blood. She raised her hand, touching her lip. In all their years together, Katherine had never once hit her. In fact, she couldn't remember them ever really fighting. But now, the look in Katherine's eyes scared her.

"Yes, I am *always* in control, Jay. Don't forget that." She pushed Jay out of the way, picking up her purse. "Yes, I slept with Jenna. It was fabulous. Something I'm sure you know nothing about. Good sex." She laughed. "And surely you don't think she was the only one, do you? There were countless others over the years. I've had many lovers. You weren't really one of them, Jay. You were never in my league, darling. You were always second-class."

To say she was stunned was an understatement. "Then why? Why did you stay?"

Katherine squared her shoulders. "I felt sorry for you, that's all. But no more. I'm done with you. I want you out of my house. I want you out of my sight."

Jay rubbed her cheek again. "All these wasted years, Katherine. I should have left you so long ago."

"Left *me*? That's a joke." She went to the door. "I've had enough of this. Enough of *you*. I can't possibly stay another three days in Hawaii. Because frankly, Jay, you do nothing but bring me down."

The door slammed hard as she left. Jay closed her eyes, her head dropping heavily to her chest. She was surprised by the stinging of tears. She wiped them away angrily. She would *not* shed a tear for that woman.

No, but she could cry for herself. And she did, finally sinking down onto the sofa, tears falling easily as she made no effort to stop them. Wasted years. How many affairs had Katherine had? Five? Ten?

She leaned forward, resting her arms on her knees, taking deep breaths, angry at herself for her tears. It wasn't worth it. But it still stung. How blind had she been? How *trusting*? It had never occurred to her that Katherine had slept around. *Second-class*. Yeah, that's exactly how Katherine had treated her. Never worthy.

"Why the hell did you stay eight years?" She shook her head. She had no answer. Had she stayed out of a sense of duty? Had she been hanging on to hope that a love would grow? Had she simply been content? Maybe all of those. Or maybe she stayed because she felt she wasn't worthy and was grateful Katherine wanted her. At least someone did.

She rolled her eyes at that thought. If she didn't stop, she would be attending her own pity party alone. And she neither wanted, nor needed pity.

She looked up at the rapid knocking on the door.

"Room service. Champagne."

She laughed quietly. "Champagne. How ironic." She stood, going to the door.

"Where would you like it?"

"At the bar is fine." She went to her purse, but she had no cash. She looked up apologetically. "Only plastic. I'll be sure to put a generous tip on the room tab."

He bowed politely. "Not a problem, ma'am. Thank you."

She closed the door with a grin. "Yes, Katherine will be *happy* to leave a large tip." She fingered the cork, nearly popping it right there in a fit of defiance. But then she dutifully took the towel he'd left and covered the top as she eased the cork out with an anticlimactic thud. She filled both of the glasses, then took one.

"Here's to me, to better days." She held the glass up in a salute before drinking. She smiled. The champagne was excellent. It was only then that she looked in the mirror behind the bar. She looked frightful. Her eyes were red and puffy, her cheek and lip swollen. "Damn." She stared in the mirror, watching her tongue come out and lightly touch her lip, the blood from the tiny cut now dry. War wounds. *Oh, well*. It is what it is. With that, she refilled her glass, taking it with her to the balcony. The breeze was warm, the sun having chased the clouds from the sky. It was a beautiful day and she had the room for the night. She could just stay.

But no. She didn't want to stay. She wanted to see Drew. She went back inside, getting her phone from her purse. She scrolled through her numbers, finding Eleu's. It rang six times before she picked up.

"It's me. Jay."

"Yes, Jay. Is everything fine?"

Jay laughed. "No, not fine. I'm at some hotel. Katherine left me here. I could call a cab, I suppose, but—"

"No, no. I will send Manko. Where are you?"

Jay looked around. "I'm not sure. It's two towers with a court-yard type thing between them."

"Yes, yes. You are at the Twin Palms. I will send Manko."

"Eleu? Is Drew around?"

"No. Drew and Jenna went out. An island cruise."

"Oh. I see."

"She was . . . she was upset, so . . ." her voice trailed off.

"Upset? Why?"

"You left with Katherine. You left no word with anyone."

"And she thought I . . . oh, no." Jay shook her head. "Katherine and I ended things. We had a . . . a fight. And she left."

"Are you okay?"

Jay touched her puffy cheek. "Yeah, I'm okay."

"Well, I will send Manko to get you."

"Thanks, Eleu."

She folded her phone shut and sat there quietly for a moment. Why had she just left with Katherine without telling anyone? What was she thinking? Truth was, she wasn't thinking of anything or anyone other than what she was going to talk to

Katherine about, what she wanted to tell Katherine. As it ended up, she didn't really tell Katherine anything.

Katherine had told her.

Second-class.

Jay touched her cheek again. Katherine was right about one thing. Jay certainly wasn't in her league. She'd hadn't yet been reduced to hitting.

CHAPTER THIRTY-FOUR

Drew pulled the cap lower on her head and leaned back in the chair. She was brooding. She knew she was, but she couldn't seem to get the image of Jay and Katherine out of her mind. Was Katherine *wooing* her, as Jenna had suggested?

"Hey."

Drew slid her sunglasses down her nose, looking over the top of them at Jenna.

"You're not much fun, are you?"

Drew let out a heavy breath. "Sorry. I guess I'm not so much fun today, no."

"She got to you, huh?"

"What do you mean?"

"Jay. You spent all that time with her. You didn't do anything stupid like fall in love with her, did you?"

Drew wanted to laugh it off, but couldn't. She shoved the

sunglasses back on her nose, turning her gaze to the rocky shore-line they were passing. "Yeah," she finally said. "I did something stupid."

"Seriously?"

Drew nodded. "Seriously."

Jenna nudged her arm. "No offense, but I don't think you can compete with Katherine."

"How so?"

"Well, I know you own your own business and all, but it hardly ranks with being one of the up-and-coming attorneys in the city. And, my God, you saw her house. It's a mansion. Of course, I don't know where you live. I've never seen your house. But like I said, no offense."

Drew's eyes narrowed. "What makes you think any of those things matter to Jay?"

Jenna shrugged. "Why wouldn't they? Besides, Katherine says Jay's little business is just a hobby for her, something to keep her busy. Katherine doubts she can actually make a living at it."

"You're kidding, right? She's really talented."

Jenna laughed. "Sorry. I really don't know anything about the decorating business. I only know Katherine said she wasn't good enough to decorate their own home. That should tell you some-thing."

Drew couldn't *believe* Katherine was so callous. Or maybe she could. It's the same woman who had an affair with Jenna, and who now was at some fancy hotel wooing Jay. *That* was what she couldn't believe.

"But Jay seems really nice. Down-to-earth. And I hate to say this, but she probably deserves someone better than Katherine."

"What do you mean?"

"I guess it took spending so much time with Katherine to learn, but she's so shallow."

Drew laughed. "You think?"

"Money, prestige . . . power. That's all that matters to her. She wasn't like that when I knew her in college. She still had scruples back then. Now, all she talks about is screwing over the firm she works for, how she's going to take their clients with her when she starts her own firm."

"Do attorneys *have* scruples?"

"I like to think I do." She shrugged. "She wants me to come work for her. The money would be great, but do I really want her for a boss? She's ruthless."

"Even after all this, she still wants you to work for her?"

Jenna nodded. "Our affair was just that, nothing more. There were no emotional strings, you know." Jenna paused. "Even though I hate where I am now, I'm just not sure I want to subject myself to all that."

They were quiet for a moment, then Jenna nudged her arm again. "So, you fell in love with her, huh?"

Drew smiled. "Afraid so."

"Yeah. You'd make a cute couple." Jenna grinned. "How does Jay feel about *you*?"

If she'd been asked this question last night—or even this morning—she'd have had an answer. But now? She sighed. "I'm not really sure."

But that was a lie, wasn't it? *I'm going to love you to death.* She closed her eyes for a second, remembering Jay's words, hoping they were true.

CHAPTER THIRTY-FIVE

Jay paused outside the cottage, hearing Katherine's angry voice. It sounded like she was arguing with the airline. Jay raised her eyebrows. So when Katherine said she couldn't stay in Hawaii for another three days, she apparently meant it.

Good.

But, after consuming nearly half a bottle of very expensive champagne, Jay's only wish was to slip into a swimsuit and relax by the pool. Where hopefully Carlos was on duty. So she pushed open the door, ignoring Katherine who was talking—yelling—animatedly on the phone. She closed the door to the bedroom, not really surprised to see Katherine's luggage spread out on the bed. That, too, she ignored as she quickly shed her clothes and pulled on the red one-piece she had yet to wear. She found the matching wind shorts, slipped them over her suit and grabbed a towel.

But when she left the bedroom, Katherine was waiting.

"I see you found a ride."

Jay stopped. "Oh, yes. That was very sweet of you to leave me there. I appreciate it."

Katherine came closer. "You didn't really think I was going to ride back with you, did you?" she asked with a smile. "You cut your lip." Their eyes met. "I hope it wasn't too painful."

Jay squared her shoulders. "You mean your assault? No. The champagne helped ease the pain." She gave her own smile. "And really, the hundred dollar tip you ended up leaving was a bit much, even for you."

Katherine laughed. "That's the best you could do with my credit card? A hundred bucks? In eight years, did I not teach you anything about spending money?"

Jay shook her head. "Whatever." She walked around Katherine, heading to the door. She had no desire to spend another second with her.

"Yeah, whatever," Katherine mimicked. "By the way, I'm leaving. Or should I say Jenna and I are leaving. I got two of the tickets changed. It cost a small fortune, but I hardly care. I would have paid twice that just to get away from here."

Jay smiled. "Great. Then don't let me keep you." She turned to go but Katherine grabbed her arm, stopping her.

"When you get back to Austin, you'll have one day to get your things out of my house, Jay. After that, you're not welcome there."

"One day? I'll need more than one day."

"Oh, I'm sure you can manage." Her smile was saccharine. "It's not like you have a lot there anyway."

Jay couldn't tell if she was serious or not. Most likely she was. "So you're just basically throwing me out on the street?"

"It's my house, Jay. Not yours." Her eyes narrowed. "I don't want you around. Get your things and get out."

"Wow, Kath. I think you've actually reached a new low." She

touched her cheek. "After this morning, I didn't think it was possible."

"Get out, Jay," she spat, pointing to the door. "I don't want to see you again."

Jay nodded. "With pleasure." But as the door slammed behind her, the calmness she'd displayed inside left her. "The bitch!"

Now what?

She took a deep breath. The buzz the champagne left her with was quickly fading, a headache taking its place. Then she saw Eleu straightening the chairs out by the pool. She headed her way. Perhaps a therapy session was in order.

"Got a second?"

Eleu smiled. "Yes. I see you made it." She looked around conspiratorially. "Where's the wicked witch?"

Jay laughed. "Making plans to fly out of here on her broom. Apparently she's taking Jenna with her."

"She's leaving?"

"Yes. She got two tickets out tomorrow."

"So . . . this means you and Drew will be here alone for a couple more days?"

"I guess, unless she cancelled those tickets. Which I wouldn't put past her." Jay waved at Carlos. "Thank God he's here." She nodded as he held up the margarita shaker. "Say, is the bar tab still on Katherine's credit card?"

"She hasn't asked me to pull it."

"Let's hope she forgets."

"Ah, you are being sneaky. Good."

Jay pulled a chair into the shade, waiting as Carlos made her drink. "It started out with me breaking up with Katherine. It ended with Katherine kicking me out of her house without my belongings. I knew she would twist it around. I just knew it. I'm not in her league. I'm second-class," she said sarcastically, as she reached for the glass. "Thanks, Carlos. You're a doll."

213

"My pleasure, as always, Miss Jay."

When he left them, Eleu sat down next to Jay, watching her. "It's none of my business, of course. But your cheek, it looks puffy. Your lip, there is a cut."

Jay nodded. "I never saw it coming."

"She hit you?"

"Twice." Jay leaned her head back. "I never thought she would stoop to that level, but I guess it shows I never really knew her that well. I wouldn't have thought she'd be this vindictive, this *mean*."

"Then perhaps it is all for the best."

"You mean with Drew?"

Eleu nodded. "Dinner was good last night, yes?"

Jay laughed. "You are quite the little matchmaker. And since you cleaned up, you know how far we got with dinner."

"My grandmother used to tell me that when love found you, it would come fast and hard. There would be no running. I think that is true for you. There was just no more running, was there?"

"No." Jay sighed. "I really like her a lot."

"But?"

"I just feel like my life's in chaos right now. I'm soon to be homeless, yet here I am, sitting in paradise, waiting for my knight in shining armor to come back from a romantic dinner cruise with another woman."

Eleu reached over and patted her leg. "Drew was crushed. And jealous. And all those other things that come with the uncertainty of a new relationship."

"I didn't mean to just leave like that. I just wanted to get alone somewhere where we could talk, that's all. Imagine my surprise when we ended up at a hotel. I mean, she hasn't wanted to spend any time with me this whole trip. Why now?"

Eleu stared at her. "Why do you think, Jay?"

"I don't know." Jay shrugged. "Maybe she got tired of museums. Maybe she . . ." Jay frowned. "Or maybe she got tired of

Jenna. Jesus, I'm so clueless sometimes, I swear." She sat up. "That's why she had the hotel. That's why she wanted to get alone with me. Christ, that's why she said she wanted to see me in a *bikini*." She laughed. "Did you know?"

"Just from watching them together at breakfast, yes, something was different. And for Jenna to want to take Drew away, I knew something had changed."

Jay's eyes widened. "Take her away? Do you think Jenna now wants *Drew*?"

"Well, that hardly matters now, does it? Because Drew doesn't want Jenna."

Jay sat back again, swirling the ice in her glass. "You seem to know an awful lot, Eleu. How old are you anyway? Are you even thirty?"

Eleu's laugh was loud and rich, her eyes crinkling at the corners. "*Thirty?* I passed thirty twelve years ago."

"Oh, my God! You're forty-two?" It was Jay's turn to laugh. "What's your secret? I had you pegged for mid-twenties."

"I do what my mother did before me, and what my grandmother did before her. I live a stress-free life, I eat well, I don't smoke or drink," she said, motioning to Jay's glass. "And I swim every morning before daybreak, rain or shine. My grandmother claimed the salt in the ocean cleansed your skin." She touched both her cheeks. "I don't wear makeup to clog my pores. I let them breathe." She laughed. "There, my family secret to aging."

Jay set her empty drink aside. "No wonder. Drew and I were commenting last night that you were old and wise." She grinned. "I don't mean old as in *old*, you know. But wise."

Eleu nodded. "Then thank you for the compliment." She got to her feet, looking down at Jay. "People live their lives in such a rush, always trying to do things faster and faster, never taking the time to really live. Don't rush through your life, Jay. Even with Drew. You have something there. You both know it. Take the time to savor it." She bowed slightly. "I will ensure you enjoy

215

these last few days in peace."

"Thank you."

Jay watched her leave, her small body lithe and firm, belying her age. Ten years older. Ten years wiser. *There's hope for me yet.* And when Carlos got her attention, asking for another drink, Jay shook her head. No, she didn't need alcohol to numb her pain.

She opened her cell phone, feeling only slightly guilty at the dozen or so messages she had yet to listen to. She reasoned she was on vacation. And she was in Hawaii. Anything going on in Austin would have to wait. But this could not.

"Audrey? It's me."

"Well, my, my. The little mermaid has surfaced."

"Very funny." She paused. "I need a therapy session."

"Oh, good Lord. You're several time zones away. Surely not."

Jay heard rustling and frowned. "Where are you?"

"In bed."

"Who with?" she asked in a whisper, only to hear Audrey's familiar laugh.

"I'm alone. Unfortunately."

"What time is it there?"

"Early. Not even nine."

"What the hell is wrong with you?"

"I'm exhausted. And if you must know, I spent the night with someone last night. We didn't exactly sleep, if you know what I mean."

"Slut."

"I know you're just jealous."

Jay laughed. "Well, I spent the night with someone too."

"I do not want to hear about your boring married life."

Jay's smile vanished. "Speaking of that, do you still have the alarm code for the house?"

"The mansion? Yes. Why?"

"Because I need you to go there and pack up my stuff."

Silence. Then, a sigh.

"Do I want to know what's going on?"

"Probably not. But Katherine and Jenna are having an affair. Or they were. Not quite sure what's up with that now. And I slept with Drew."

"Oh, my God! You slut!" Audrey shrieked, then squealed with laughter. "Tell me more."

"Today Katherine took me to a fancy hotel to have makeup sex. I broke up with her. She's plenty pissed. She's leaving in the morning and—"

"Wait, wait, wait. You broke up with her?"

"Yes. But since she's kicking me out of the house, she's technically the one breaking up with me. Which is fine. I don't care."

"Are you okay?"

"Yes, I'm fine. I'm relieved, actually."

"And she's leaving tomorrow?"

"Yes. She got two tickets changed. She and Jenna are both leaving."

Another laugh. "And you and Drew are staying?"

"I suppose. Right now, Drew and Jenna are on a romantic dinner cruise of the islands."

"Oh, my God! My head is spinning."

"Yes, well, so is mine. Katherine is as pissed as I've ever seen her."

"Because you slept with Drew? But if she was having her own affair—"

"No. She doesn't know about Drew."

"How can she not know? Why did she think you wanted to end things with her?"

Jay rubbed her forehead. This was too much for a phone call. She should have known Audrey would have a hundred questions. "Look, she's just pissed because I found out about her and Jenna, that's the main thing. And she's, you know, *pissed*. And so she got kinda ugly with me, and well, I don't want to go into it. I'll explain it all when I get back. But I *need* you to get my stuff. If I can help it, I'd rather not have to go over there when we get back."

"So you want me to break in?"

"If you know the alarm code, is that really breaking in?"

"Okay, I guess not."

"Great. Park in the back by the garage and use the patio door. Put whatever you can into my van. I've got to have my computer. Basically, everything that's in my office. And if you forget my Cowboys mini helmet I'll never speak to you again."

"Yeah, yeah. So, get your stuff in your office. What clothes do you want?"

"Just whatever you can get. Shorts, jeans. Whatever. Forget the stuff in the closet. Most of that is what Katherine bought me whenever I needed to dress up for one of her functions." Jay thought for a moment, trying to picture anything else she couldn't live without. "I'm assuming you can get someone to go with you to drive my van, right?"

"I'll find someone. You'll want to bunk with me for awhile, I suppose?"

"If you don't mind."

"Of course not. It'll be fun."

"Just for a week or so. Until I find something." She smiled. "I love you, you know."

"Yeah. Me too. I just hope this doesn't cut into my social life."

"Sex with strangers is not considered a social life, Audrey." She laughed. "But there *is* a word for that."

"If you don't want me to put your precious little mini helmet on eBay, I'd be careful what you call me, *Jessica*."

Jay laughed delightfully, having missed the teasing banter between them. "I'm so sorry. You're the best, Audrey."

"Much better. Now, I'm going back to bed to plan my heist in the morning. And Jay, if I get arrested for breaking and entering . . . I will kill you. And I will kill you slowly."

Jay leaned back in her lounge chair, a smile still on her face.

Audrey always made her feel better, always made her laugh. And was always there when she needed her. So maybe it wouldn't be so bad. At least she'd have her stuff. And now Katherine would be gone and she and Drew would have two days to . . . to what?

To talk? To make plans? To decide the direction of their relationship?

"To make love," she murmured quietly, letting her eyes close, remembering—for the first time that day—Drew's hands upon her skin, Drew's mouth upon her breast. Her body had come alive, responding to Drew's touch like never before. Drew made her feel beautiful, sexy. She lost all her inhibitions when she was with Drew. She became the physical, *passionate l*over she always wanted to be, always knew she was.

Not with Katherine, no. With Katherine it was always so civilized, so restrained. There was never any urgency, there was never any ripping off of their clothes. There wasn't any *passion*.

But with Drew, there was that crazy, crazy need to touch and be touched that drove her to heights she'd never reached before.

Because Drew made her feel *alive*.

CHAPTER THIRTY-SIX

Drew rode with the window open, her arm hanging out, her fingers impatiently tapping the side of the car. It had been a very long day and she was more than ready for it to come to an end. The island dinner cruise, while nice, would have been much more enjoyable had Jay been her company instead of Jenna.

"Your tapping is not going to get us there any quicker."

"Sorry."

"And I don't know why you're in such a rush. I told you they were staying at a hotel tonight."

Drew shook her head. "And I told you that wasn't going to happen."

"I hope for your sake you're right, but don't hold your breath. Katherine is *very* persuasive."

Perhaps. But Drew had been over the whole thing a dozen times in her mind. And she knew in her heart that Jay would not stay with Katherine tonight. And what had finally convinced her wasn't necessarily Jay's words to her, but the look in her eyes. That morning, out on the beach, when Jay had looked at her, it was all there. Anyone could utter words, but that didn't mean they really *meant* them. But Jay . . . she had turned those blue eyes on her and Drew had seen everything she wanted—needed—to see. Her eyes were honest. Her eyes were true. And her eyes were filled with love. Love for her.

And if she hadn't forgotten her phone, hadn't left it hidden in a drawer, she could have called. But then Jay's phone was probably also still hidden, a pact they'd made on their first day there, a pact to leave their cell phones behind so they wouldn't be bothered.

"And what exactly are you going to do if Jay's not there? Are you going to crash their hotel room?"

"She'll be there."

"Well, I'll say this, you don't lack for confidence."

Drew turned, smiling. "We were . . . we were together last night," she said.

"Together?" She raised an eyebrow. "You mean *together*? Sex?"

Drew nodded.

"You devil." Then she laughed. "How ironic. Katherine is sneaking off with me thinking Jay doesn't have a clue and Jay is having her own affair. Isn't that hilarious?"

"Yeah, just hilarious."

"Katherine is going to be *so* pissed."

Drew shrugged. "She has no right to be pissed."

"Oh, I agree. But that's hardly going to matter." Jenna laughed again. "This could really be fun."

Drew pointed up ahead. "Slow down. You're going to miss the turn."

"Sorry."

The light had all but faded from the sky but the long driveway to the cottages was well-lit. Jenna parked near the office and Drew bounded out of the car, impatiently waiting as Jenna gathered her things.

They went through the courtyard behind the office, the pool and garden area still humming with activity. They both stopped up short as Katherine walked quickly toward them.

"About time," she snapped. "Do you *not* have your cell?" she asked Jenna.

"Oh, sorry. I turned it off during the tour. I forgot to turn it back on."

"Well, whatever. We're leaving."

Drew's eyebrows shot up. "Leaving?"

"Not you. Jenna and I. You, unfortunately, are stuck here with Jay." She squared her shoulders. "I'm leaving her."

Jenna glanced quickly at Drew, then back to Katherine. "What's going on?"

"I have finally gotten her out of my life, that's what is going on. We've got a flight out in the morning."

"Where is Jay?" Drew asked.

"Perhaps she went into the ocean and drowned . . . I don't care. I'm just glad to be rid of her. She did nothing but bring me down. She's the most negative—*miserable*—person I've ever met."

"*Jay?*" Drew shook her head. "You obviously don't know her very well."

Katherine laughed. "Oh, I know her plenty. She may have put on a good show for you this past week, but I *know* her. She's a gold-digger, a leech. She brought nothing to this relationship. Nothing. She was an embarrassment to me." She turned to Jenna. "Come on, sweetheart. I have a wonderful hotel picked out for us. We don't have to pretend any longer. Your things are already packed and in Manko's car."

Drew saw the surprised—and confused—look that crossed Jenna's face. It all became very clear to her then. Jay's presence in

Katherine's life was one of convenience, to be used however Katherine saw fit. When the affair with Jenna ended, Katherine did what she always did . . . turned on the charm with Jay, trying to smooth things over. Only this time, Jay wouldn't be swayed. This time, Jay wanted to end things. And Katherine did exactly what Jay predicted she'd do. She turned things around, making Jay out to be the horrible beast in all this. And now, since Katherine thought she still had the upper hand, she was pretending, at least in front of Drew, that she and Jenna were still hot and heavy in their affair. She smiled, wondering if Jenna would confess that she'd already spilled the beans. Oh, well. She didn't care one way or the other. She only cared about Jay.

"My things are packed? *Everything?*"

"Yes, dear. We're all set." She nodded at Drew. "Sorry to leave you here alone, but it's only for a few days."

Drew managed to keep the silly grin off her face as she returned the curt nod. "No problem. I've enjoyed it here. Thank you." She turned to Jenna. "Have a good trip back."

"Well, I don't suppose we'll be seeing each other again." She offered her hand. "It's been fun."

"For sure."

Drew watched them hurry through the courtyard, amused at Katherine's haste. But *so* thankful they were gone.

"About time you come back."

Drew turned, smiling at Eleu. "Where is she?"

"She is out on the beach."

"Is she okay?"

Eleu nodded. "I imagine she is waiting for you."

Drew glanced over her shoulder, seeing Manko drive away with Katherine and Jenna. "Very strange trip."

Eleu laughed. "I can honestly say it has been the *strangest*, yes." She grasped both of Drew's arms. "I am very glad they are gone. I will make sure the next few days are memorable for you." She winked. "And I will move Jay's things into your cottage. Is that okay?"

"Yes, please."

"Good. Now go to her. She waits."

Drew cocked her head. "Got a couple of towels I can borrow?"

Eleu's lips twitched in a smile. "You may take some from the pool house."

Drew hurried away, then tossed back over her shoulder, "I can't promise you'll get them back."

CHAPTER THIRTY-SEVEN

Jay stood in the surf, her head tilted up, staring at the full moon. Now that the initial shock was over, now that she'd had time to sort through everything, she couldn't believe how relieved she was. The heavy, heavy weight she'd been carrying around was gone. She was free.

And the possibilities were endless. She was finally at a point in her life where *she* was in control. Not her parents, as they'd been when they chased her from her home. Not Wilkes and Bonner as they milked her for her talent with very little pay. And now certainly not Katherine, who'd been controlling every facet of her life since she was twenty-four.

No, now she was free. She had her own business and she didn't have to answer to anyone. Free. Free to be who she was. Free to just be *Jay*.

She laughed, the sound disappearing into the surf as the wind carried it away. *Free.* She held her arms out to her side, letting the wind blow through her, cleansing her, chasing away the last of the façade she'd held in place.

God, it feels good.

Yeah, it did.

She turned and walked down the beach, slowly, feeling the surf nip at her feet, enjoying the solitude. She had a ton of things to think about, a ton of planning to do, but that could wait, she decided. Now, for the next few days, she just wanted to be with Drew. She didn't want to *talk* about it. She just wanted to *be.* When they got back to Austin, then they could talk.

She stopped again, taking a deep breath, turning her face again to the moon . . . and waited.

But she didn't have to wait long. She didn't hear Drew, but she felt her presence . . . or did she smell her, *see* her? Regardless, Drew was here. Finally. So she stood still, waiting. And then she felt her move behind her, felt Drew's arms wrap around her, pulling her back into her solid frame. They didn't speak. Jay laid her head back against Drew's shoulder and they stood there in silence, breathing the same ocean air, feeling the same wind as it danced around them, tossing their hair about their faces, hearing the same surf as it rushed to shore and then back out again . . . and listening to the same steady beats of their hearts. There was nothing to say except—

"I love you."

She felt Drew's arms tighten around her, felt Drew's breath against her ear, felt her lips as they caressed her cheek. "Are you okay?"

Jay nodded. "Yes. I'm . . . I'm good."

"You want to talk about it?"

"No. It's over."

Drew stepped away and turned Jay around to face her, the moonlight shining bright upon her face. Jay saw her brows furrow, saw the concerned look on her face. Drew touched her puffy cheek, her thumb gently rubbing across her lip. Then her eyes narrowed and she opened her mouth to speak, but Jay silenced her, placing her finger against Drew's lips.

"I'm okay. Really. It just reinforced everything, that's all."

"I just can't—"

"No. I don't want to talk about it. I just want it to be *us*. Just you and me. Just a couple of days of . . . of us."

Drew stared at her for a long moment, finally nodding. Jay saw the understanding there and was grateful. Tonight, she didn't want to talk about Katherine. Tonight, Katherine didn't exist.

Drew stepped back away from her, a grin on her face. "You know, this whole trip, Carlos has made me every fruity drink under the sun. I've had a mai tai, a piña colada, a Hawaiian sunset, a blue Hawaii—that was a good one—"

"Rum runner," Jay recalled, wondering why Drew was listing off drinks *now*.

"Yeah. I forgot about that." She laughed, pulling Jay into her arms again. "But I haven't had the one I was most looking forward to."

"What's that?" Jay asked, not knowing where Drew was going with this.

She arched her eyebrows teasingly, then bent to Jay's ear, her lips moving enticingly close before whispering, "Sex on the beach."

Jay laughed delightfully. "Oh, my God! You're not serious?"

Drew took her hand and pulled her into the shadows, finding the two towels she'd tossed to the sand. "Of course I am."

Jay moved into her arms, reveling in the gentle kisses Drew gave her, finally opening her mouth, letting Drew inside. It seemed like an eternity since last night, since this morning when they'd touched. She closed her eyes with a satisfied moan as Drew's hands moved up her body, boldly cupping her breasts, her fingers teasing her nipples.

"Mmm," she murmured. "You know, if we get busted for this," she said, "I'll—"

"You'll what?" Drew whispered against her mouth.

Jay pulled back, staring into her eyes. She shook her head with a smile. "I've never had sex on the beach."

Drew's hands moved under Jay's shirt, touching her flesh, making her tremble. Drew bent her head, placing a light, delicate kiss on her lips. Jay closed her eyes, loving Drew's gentleness.

"I love you so much, Jay," Drew said, her mouth moving slowly across Jay's face, her lips caressing her skin. "It's going to be good with us. I think . . . I think it's going to be really good."

"Yeah." Jay's arms tightened around Drew, pulling their bodies into a tight embrace. "Yeah, it's going to be great with us."

Publications from
BELLA BOOKS, INC.
The best in contemporary lesbian fiction

P.O. Box 10543, Tallahassee, FL 32302
Phone: 800-729-4992
www.bellabooks.com

WHISKEY AND OAK LEAVES by Jaime Clevenger. Meg meets June, a single woman running a horse ranch in the California Sierra foothills. The two become quick friends and it isn't long before Meg is looking for more than just a friendship. But June has no interest in developing a deeper relationship with Meg. She is, after all, not the least bit interested in women . . . or is she? Neither of these two women is prepared for what lies ahead . . .   978-1-59493-093-5 $13.95

SUMTER POINT by KG MacGregor. As Audie surrenders her heart to Beth, she begins to distance herself from the reckless habits of her youth. Just as they're ready to meet in the middle, their future is thrown into doubt by a duty Beth can't ignore. It all comes to a head on the river at Sumter Point.   978-1-59493-089-8 $13.95

THE TARGET by Gerri Hill. Sara Michaels is the daughter of a prominent senator who has been receiving death threats against his family. In an effort to protect Sara, the FBI recruits homicide detective Jaime Hutchinson to secretly provide the protection they are so certain Sara will need. Will Sara finally figure out who is behind the death threats? And will Jaime realize the truth—and be able to save Sara before it's too late?
978-1-59493-082-9 $13.95

REALITY BYTES by Jane Frances. In this sequel to *Reunion*, follow the lives of four friends in a romantic tale that spans the globe and proves that you can cross the whole of cyberspace only to find love a few suburbs away . . .   978-1-59493-079-9 $13.95

MURDER CAME SECOND by Jessica Thomas. Broadway's bad-boy genius, Paul Carlucci, has chosen *Hamlet* for his latest production and, to the delight of some and despair of others, he has selected Provincetown's amphitheatre for his opening gala. But Alex Peres realizes the wrong people are falling down, and the moaning is all too realistic. Someone must not be shooting blanks . . .   978-1-59493-081-2 $13.95

SKIN DEEP by Kenna White. Jordan Griffin has been given a new assignment: Track down and interview one-time nationally renowned broadcast journalist Reece McAllister. Much to her surprise, Jordan comes away with far more than just a story . . .
978-1-59493-78-2 $13.95

FINDERS KEEPERS by Karin Kallmaker. *Finders Keepers*, the quest for the perfect mate in the 21st century, joins Karin Kallmaker's *Just Like That* and her other incomparable novels about lesbian love, lust and laughter.   1-59493-072-4 $13.95

OUT OF THE FIRE by Beth Moore. Author Ann Covington feels at the top of the world when told her book is being made into a movie. Then in walks Casey Duncan the actress who is playing the lead in her movie. Will Casey turn Ann's world upside down?
1-59493-088-0 $13.95

STAKE THROUGH THE HEART: NEW EXPLOITS OF TWILIGHT LESBIANS by Karin Kallmaker, Julia Watts, Barbara Johnson and Therese Szymanski. The playful quartet that penned the acclaimed *Once Upon A Dyke* are dimming the lights for journeys into worlds of breathless seduction.   1-59493-071-6 $15.95

THE HOUSE ON SANDSTONE by KG MacGregor. Carly Griffin returns home to Leland and finds that her old high school friend Justine is awakening more than just old memories.   1-59493-076-7 $13.95

WILD NIGHTS: MOSTLY TRUE STORIES OF WOMEN LOVING WOMEN edited by Therese Szymanski. 264 pp. 23 new stories from today's hottest erotic writers are sure to give you your wildest night ever!   1-59493-069-4 $15.95